JO ANN YHARD

BURIED SECRETS *at* LOUISBOURG

NIMBUS
PUBLISHING

Nimbus Publishing Limited
3731 Mackintosh St, Halifax, NS B3K 5A5
(902) 455-4286 nimbus.ca

Printed and bound in Canada

Author photo: Rhonda Basden
Cover design: Heather Bryan
Interior design: Heather Bryan

Library and Archives Canada Cataloguing in Publication

Yhard, Jo Ann
Buried secrets at Louisbourg / Jo Ann Yhard.
Issued also in electronic formats.
ISBN 978-1-77108-018-7

I. Title.

PS8647.H37B87 2013 jC813'.6 C2012-907370-9

Nimbus Publishing acknowledges the financial support for its publishing activities from the Government of Canada through the Canada Book Fund (CBF) and the Canada Council for the Arts, and from the Province of Nova Scotia through the Department of Communities, Culture and Heritage.

For James, my husband and best friend

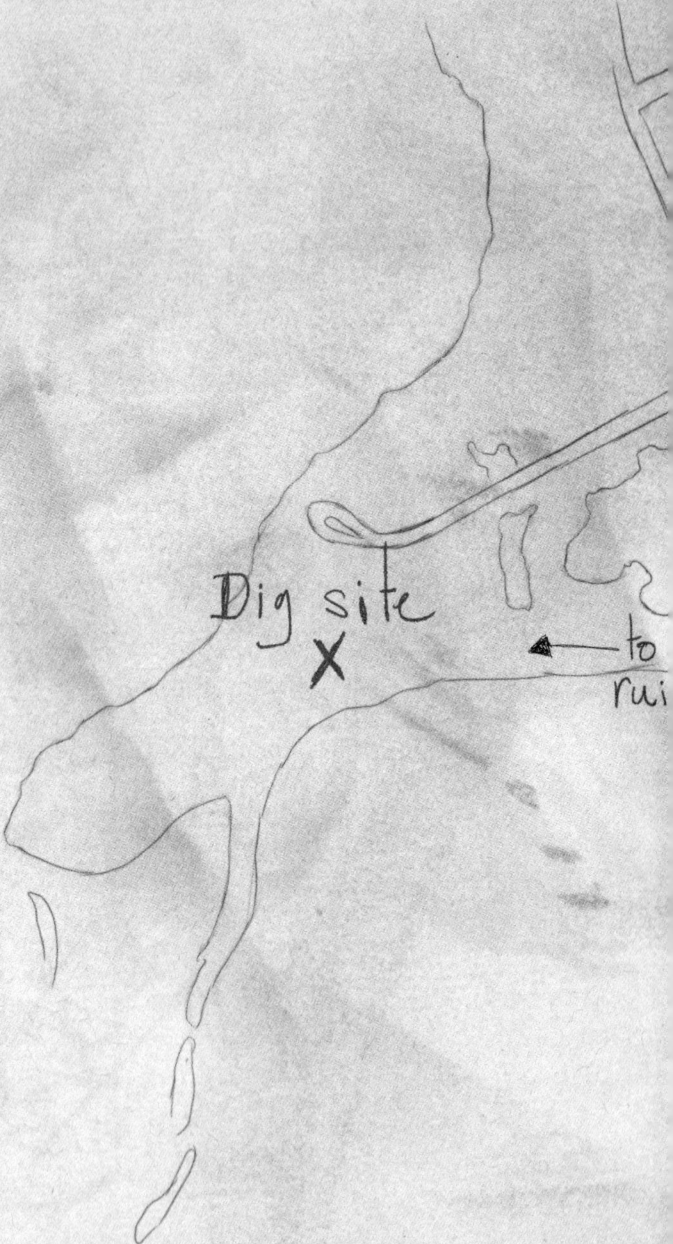

Dig site
X
to
rui

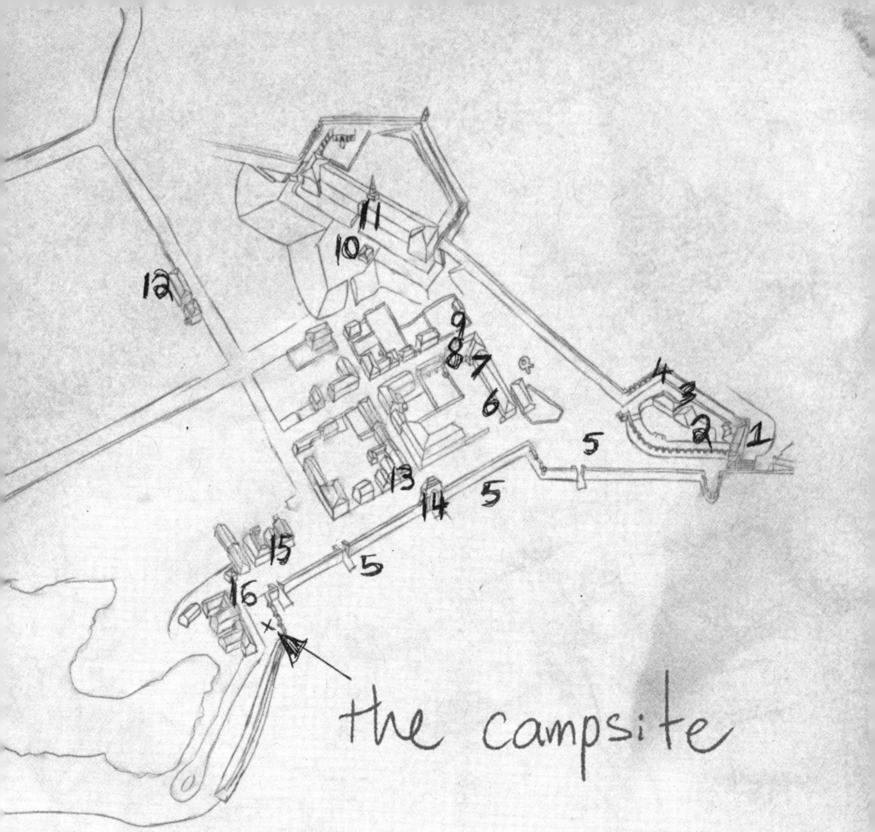

Legend

1. Dauphin Gate
2. Dauphin demi-bastion
3. Barracks
4. Powder magazine
5. The Quay
6. Artillery Forge
7. Artillery Bakery
8. Kings Bakery
9. Armoury and Forge
10. Guardhouse
11. Kings Bastion barracks
12. Museum
13. Grandchamp House (Restaurant)
14. Frédéric Gate
15. Beauséjour House-"Le Billard"
16. Chevalier House

Chapter 1

FRED GRABBED THE SPADE AND plunged it into the damp earth. It felt good to dig. The sun was hot on his back, but the ocean breeze was cool. He couldn't believe he was finally here.

"What exactly are we doing here again?" Grace asked, lifting her head.

"Digging."

"No kidding, *Freddo*," Grace said. She flicked a spade full of dirt in his direction. "Digging for what?"

"I'll know it when I see it." Carefully, he sifted another handful of dirt through his fingers.

"Why the mystery?" Mai asked.

"I can't tell you yet. You guys have to trust me."

Mai sat back on her heels, brushing the hair out of her face. A strand was stuck to the corner of her bottom lip.

Fred watched her blow it gently away. He gulped as her eyes met his, feeling heat flood his cheeks.

"Of course we trust you, Freddo." She smiled. "But if we knew what we were looking for, we might find it faster."

That's me, he thought, *good ol' Freddo. She always looks at me the same way—like I'm some lost puppy dog.* "Just show me whatever you find, okay?"

Grace muttered under her breath, but resumed digging. Mai shifted another pile of dirt out of her way. Fred remained silent. He had no choice. He *couldn't* say anything. If he told them what he was looking for, they'd think he was nuts.

He scanned the ground inside the remains of the crumbling stone foundation. It was hard to believe this had been the location of an entire house. It didn't seem much bigger than a living room. The area had already been prepared for excavation, like many other building sites in the ruins; the top layers of grass and rocks had been removed. Otherwise, digging would have been much more difficult. It was luck that this wasn't the site of today's official dig. One more indication in Fred's mind that he was meant to be here.

The King's Bastion towered over them from the top of the hill. Out here on the point, in the ruins, they were outside the reconstructed portion of the Fortress of Louisbourg. Fred, Mai, and Grace were plunk in the middle of where the main part of the town had been. Remnants of collapsed and demolished walls poked out from underneath lumpy carpets of grass and dirt.

Fred examined the collection of artifacts they'd uncovered so far. A few nails, pieces of broken plates, a metal spoon, and a cup. A pile of junk! In two hours, they had barely covered a fraction of the small space.

Time was running out.

What if he didn't find it? What if he was in the wrong place? Beads of sweat bubbled on his forehead. That wasn't an option. He had to find it.

"C'mon you guys, go faster," he growled. He had checked the map a hundred times. This was where the house had been. It *was* the right place. He attacked the ground with fury. But the digging and sifting under the hot sun lasted only a few more minutes.

"All right, that's it!" Grace threw down her spade. "We don't work for you, you know. If we did, I'd have to go on strike for better pay. Heck, for *any* pay. We've been digging in the dirt all morning and I don't even know what I'm supposed to be looking for."

Mutiny! He turned to Mai, confident of her support. Two to one—Grace would be outvoted. But he was face to face with another rebellion.

"I don't like being barked at," she said, crossing her arms. With her lips pressed into a grimace and her eyebrows mashed together in an angry line, she reminded him of a princess warrior in one of his video games—pretty, but don't cross her 'cause she'll kill you.

"Okay, okay, I'm sorry."

"Tell us what we're doing here."

"Mai, please. You guys have to help me. I can't do it by myself. We may never get back here," he begged. "C'mon, Grace."

"Fred, enough with the cloak and dagger. No games," Grace said.

"It's not a game!" he shouted. "It's my LIFE!"

"Your…life?" Grace repeated. "Are you cracking up? What are you talking about?"

Time was wasting. No one was digging. He sucked in a deep breath and blew it out slowly. Maybe he could tell them. They might even believe him.

He opened his mouth to speak when a blur of movement caught his eye. "Get down!" he rasped, dropping flat to the ground.

"What the—" Looking even more confused, Grace obeyed, sprawling in the dirt. Mai crouched down beside her, worry replacing anger in her chocolate brown eyes.

Please don't come over here. Please don't come over here. Fred's silent prayer ricocheted inside his skull like a pinball. He lifted his head a smidge, trying to catch another glimpse of the man in the soldier's uniform. He had to be a fortress employee. Where had he gone?

"Why are we hiding?" Grace whispered fiercely. "Mom said I could come this weekend to stay *out* of trouble!"

"Shhh!"

She glared at him with Medusa eyes.

Sweat trickled a lazy path between his shoulder blades. He counted—*one, two, three*—up to one hundred. Nothing. Were they safe? He rose to his knees, peering over the grassy slope that surrounded the foundation. He felt like a gopher poking out of its hole, watching for the hovering eagle to swoop down and grab him in its talons.

"Who—are—we—hiding—from?"

Grace's lips were almost touching his ear. Fred jumped and lost his balance, toppling backward against the rock wall. She advanced menacingly. He feared for a moment she actually could turn him to stone with her angry eyes. His fingers clenched, burrowing into the soft dirt beneath him.

Wait a minute. This didn't feel like dirt. It was soft and fluffy. He pulled out a handful and ground some in his palm. The residue was grey and sooty. Ash. The fireplace.

"We're not allowed to be here," Grace guessed, interrupting his thoughts. "That's why everyone else is digging further away at that roped-off place, isn't it?"

Mai's mouth fell open. "Is that true?" she gasped. "I mean, this is a heritage site. They only let the public in on this archaeological program a few days a year." She dug into her pocket, pulling out a neatly folded brochure and waving it at him. "We have permission to be on this lot, don't we, Fred? We're not breaking the law, are we?"

"Uh…" he said, digging his hands deeper into the ash. Was it possible? Could he have buried it here?

"Fred! *Could we get arrested?*"

"What?" He felt around with his fingers. How deep did the ash go? Fred pushed down harder. It was a curious sensation, being buried up to the elbows. His shoulders were pressed against the cold stone of the foundation. Grace was still glowering down at him.

"Are you listening to me?"

Mai's voice tickled his brain, as if from far away. Fred closed his eyes, his senses honed in on his fingers as they tunnelled through the ash.

"Ouch!" he cried. His index finger had run into something sharp. Gently, he felt around the area, his fingers finding the straight edges of something cool and hard...and square.

The box!

He could barely breathe. This was it. Just like he'd dreamed. Everything was going to be okay after all. His fingers curled around his find. Sighing, Fred tilted his head back and slowly opened his eyes. An angry face stared down at him.

"What do you think you're doing?" the soldier snarled.

Chapter 2

FRED GAPED UP AT THE angry soldier dressed in blue, his eyes drawn to the long gun at his side. The re-enactor's eighteenth-century French officer's uniform looked totally real, just like photos he'd seen. So what about the gun? Was it real, too?

"Well?" barked the soldier.

"I…I…"

"Cat got your tongue?"

Fred clutched the box tighter. Whatever happened, he wasn't leaving without it.

"Trying to think up a lie, eh? Out with it!"

Could my heart explode? Fred wondered, wincing as it thundered like a Japanese taiko drum in his ear. Paralyzed, he couldn't think of anything to say. He was dead meat!

"We're part of the Public Archaeological Program," Mai said.

The soldier immediately relaxed his stance. "Oh, you're with those people, are you?" he grunted, rolling his eyes. He waved his gun toward the roped-off section on the other side of the ruins. "You're supposed to be over there with the rest of them."

"Sorry," she continued. "It was so crowded, we thought it wouldn't matter which part of the ruins we excavated. As long as we turned in what we found, of course."

Fred held his breath, his arms still buried in soot.

The soldier rotated in a slow circle, examining each of them in turn. His gaze rested on the few items they'd found. "Well," he said, "it does matter. This is a protected site, and I'm here to do just that—protect it. You can't dig wherever you feel like it."

Oh great, Fred thought, *psycho soldier.* "We didn't know."

"They shouldn't be letting the public dig in here anyway," the soldier said. "I warned them it wasn't a good idea."

"We'll leave," Grace said.

"This might be just a field of rocks to you kids, but it's actually a very important place." Soldier guy stuck his chest out, his arms spread wide. "Bet you kids didn't know this—the Fortress of Louisbourg is the biggest reconstructed site in North America. A real piece of history."

"It is amazing," Mai said.

"And it needs to be protected." The soldier stood over Fred. "You. Up. You'll all have to come with me."

The guy was going to turn them in. Fred couldn't believe he'd come this close and was going to lose it all. As the soldier bent to scoop up their meagre collection of unearthed treasures, Fred glared at Grace. Distract him, he mouthed silently, his eyes darting to the soldier's back.

Grace grinned and nodded.

"Um, officer?" she cooed in a sickly sweet and very un-Grace-like voice. "Could I ask you some questions about the fortress? You seem like you know a lot." She spread out a map along the wall away from Fred.

"Well, yes, I do. I've worked here every summer for fifteen years," he said. "I know every boulder and brick."

Mai and Grace huddled over the map, asking questions about various buildings. Fred pulled the box out of the ash and leapt to his feet. He stuffed the narrow, flat, black metal case down the front of his pants and pulled his shirt out over, letting it hang loose. It seemed to hide the bulge from the box. At least, he hoped it did.

What was the punishment for removing artifacts from a heritage site? He imagined being locked away in some dungeon-like prison for fifty years, with long white hair and crazy eyes, never seeing his family again—

"Hey, kid!"

Fred snapped out of his daydream. "What?"

"Guilty conscience?"

Did he suspect? Could he see there was something under his shirt? "What? No, I—"

"We're leaving,' Grace interrupted. "No problem. We're going *right now*." She grabbed her pack and handed Fred his. "Come on," she whispered. "And walk behind me. You've got soot all over your shirt."

He could feel the sharp metal edges of the box digging

into his skin. Maybe he could sneak it into his backpack. The waist of his jeans wasn't very secure—they were baggier than ever these days.

"Hang on," the soldier said. "What's in those packs?"

"Nothing," Mai said.

"How do I know that? I'll have to take you to the office to have them searched. This is a breach of security."

"Please, we, uh, don't want to get in any trouble," Fred said. "Isn't there something you can do?"

The soldier stroked his chin. "Well," he said. "You'll have to show me what you've got in there. I wouldn't be doing my job if I just let you walk away without checking inside them."

"You can't do that," Grace said. She shoved her pack behind her back. "Isn't that like an illegal search or something?"

"Fine." The soldier shrugged. "We'll go to the security office. But they'll *still* look in your packs, and you'll probably get kicked out of here."

"No!" Fred shouted. "We're camping here—part of the grand encampment. We can't get kicked out."

"Your choice," the soldier said.

Fred pleaded to Mai and Grace with his eyes.

"Oh, fine," Grace relented, handing over her pack. "But I still think it's illegal." Mai surrendered hers as well. The soldier began rooting through them, searching every compartment and placing the contents one by one on the grass.

Mai inched over to stand beside Fred and grabbed his arm. "What are you doing?" she hissed in his ear.

"What do you mean?"

"I saw you stick something in your shirt."

"No I didn't."

She jabbed him in the stomach, her knuckle banging on the metal. "Then what's that?"

The box slipped. He grabbed the front of his jeans, catching it before it fell down his pant leg. Luckily, the soldier, still sorting through Mai's pack, had his back to them.

"Mai, don't start," Fred whispered. He wiggled around, trying to shift the box to a more secure spot.

"You aren't seriously stealing that?"

"It's not stealing," he said. "It belongs to me."

Mai's jaw dropped. "Okay, now I know you're losing it. You think something you just dug up in a three-hundred-year-old fortress belongs to *you*?"

"I know it does."

"How do you figure that?"

"It's a long story."

"Next," the soldier said, beckoning over his shoulder for Fred's backpack.

Fred was still doing a little dance to get the box over his right leg so he could hold on to it through his pocket, and trying to hide the sooty handprints on his shirt. Mai glared at him, grabbed his bag, and stomped over to pass it to the soldier.

"What are you doing with all that stuff?" The soldier pointed to the contents of Mai's bag spread out on the grass.

"I like to be prepared."

"For what? World War Three?"

"Thank you for being neat." Mai smiled and began methodically repacking her bag.

The soldier shook his head and turned to Grace. "And you," he said, "are you kidding me? Swiss Army knife, rope, gloves, *duct tape*?"

"We're explorers," she said, as if that explained everything.

He held Grace's gaze. She didn't flinch. Oh no, Fred thought. What if he changed his mind and took them to security after all? That couldn't happen.

"Uh-huh." The soldier passed her empty pack back to her.

Suddenly, another blue-uniformed employee appeared. His eyes widened as he took in the backpack contents strewn over the grass. "*Gerard!* What are you doing?"

"These kids aren't supposed to be here." He pointed to the small pile of artifacts.

"You can't search their stuff!"

"I had to make sure they didn't take anything."

The other soldier ran his hand through his hair. "You take this way too seriously, Gerard. We're just re-enactors, you know—a summer job. If there's a problem, you're supposed to tell security. That's *their* job."

"No, it's okay," Fred said. "We told him he could."

"Why would you do that?" the other soldier asked.

"It's our fault—we were in the wrong place," Fred replied. "He was giving us a break. Look, he can see what's in my bag, too. Mai, show him."

Mai dumped everything onto the grass. Fred's rumpled clothes and balled-up papers were a stark contrast to Mai's tidy pile, now neatly packed away.

The other soldier shook his head. "Whatever," he said.

Gerard reached out as if to search through the pile.

The other soldier cleared his throat. "*Gerard*."

"Well, I suppose you weren't stealing anything," Gerard said, finally. He sounded disappointed. His eyes met Fred's. "But you're up to something. There's no doubt about that."

Fred opened his mouth to protest, but Mai's warning stare stopped him.

"Give it a rest, Gerard. C'mon, kids," the other soldier said.

Fred shuffled awkwardly over to the wall, leaning against the stone to hold the box in place so he had both hands free to pack his things. The guard was surveying him with a frown.

As they marched single file along the path to join the authorized excavation site, Gerard leaned over and whispered menacingly in Fred's ear, "I'll be watching you."

Chapter 3

PSYCHO GERARD STAYED TRUE TO his word. Fred, Mai, and Grace remained with the tourists, digging for the rest of the morning and into the afternoon—all the while under his scrutiny.

They didn't have much of a choice, really. If they left after saying that this was what they had come to do, it would have seemed suspicious. Gerard could still follow through on his threat and take them to security. And security would take Fred's box.

When Gerard had refused to leave them at the site alone, the other soldier had grumbled something about Gerard getting fired if he didn't watch it, and left.

The Parks Canada archaeologist was busy directing the site, and didn't seem alarmed that they were so much younger than everyone else and had not arrived with the rest of the volunteers—or even that an eighteenth-century soldier was keeping watch over them.

Mai had said they were there for a school project and the archaeologist had nodded vaguely, waving them to a clear spot between an older man and woman. A few instructions on how to dig and screen the soil, and they were left to work away.

The volunteers were very curious about Gerard, though. They'd all arrived before official park hours, so the re-enactors hadn't been on duty. He was the first "sighting" of a soldier for those that had never visited the fortress before.

"Are you in character? Do you talk like the soldiers at the fortress would have back when it was operating?" a woman asked.

"Yes, ma'am. But we only do that at our posts in the reconstructed part of the fortress." He pointed up the hill to the buildings. "I have a shift up at the gate later."

"So what's your role?" the woman continued. "Can you tell us what it was like back then?"

Gerard seemed to love the attention. He answered endless questions about a soldier's life—from living conditions, to what his uniform was made of, and the general history of the fortress.

Despite his overall lack of interest, some of the things Fred heard shocked him. Soldiers only made seven dollars a month and took a bath once a year? *Gross!* Several slept in a bunk and there were lice and fleas in the beds, their uniforms stank, and the soldiers all froze in the winter. On top of that, they almost starved and many took on extra jobs around the fortress to buy food—like fish heads to make soup. What kind of life was that?

As he pretended to dig, Fred noticed Gerard wasn't the only one glaring at him. Grace was shooting daggers at him every few minutes. He didn't get why she was so mad—she was usually the first one with her hands in the dirt when it came to caves and fossils. You'd think this would be right up her alley. She was probably ticked because it wasn't her idea.

But Fred had worse problems than Gerard and Grace. By the middle of the afternoon, his right thigh felt like it had been shredded to hamburger by the edges of the metal box still hidden in his pants.

The situation was made even worse by the irritatingly cheery chatter around him.

"Isn't this exciting, being part of uncovering the history of this place?" a middle-aged man said. He held up a broken piece of blue and white pottery. "See this, it's French—the fleur-de-lis," he added, pointing to the blue pattern. "That's French for lily flower."

"Cool," Fred answered, carelessly flinging aside a scoop of dirt. Whoopee, more pottery. He swore under his breath as a metal edge dug a fresh trench in his leg. The box had given him nothing but pain so far. He wondered what that meant. Guess he didn't have to wait for the prison after all—he was already there. The only things missing were leg irons and a uniform.

Time oozed by like a fat slug. The metal burned hot on Fred's leg, the box taunting him with the secrets it held. He shivered, trying not to think about it. The waiting was worse than the pain. He now possessed the box he had been dreaming of for weeks and couldn't look inside. It was driving him crazy!

A dull rhythm developed, digging interspersed with pauses to examine various nails and pieces of green and blue glass they discovered. There was a bit of excitement when one person found a weird-looking contraption that no one could identify. Gerard the soldier snatched it from her before the archaeologist had a chance.

He took his time examining it, holding it one way, then another. "Ah, yes, of course," he smirked. "Quite a useful tool back in the day. An amazing discovery, madame!"

"Don't keep us in suspense," gushed the woman. "Tell us."

He waited another moment. The crowd leaned forward with anticipation. Holding it up for all to see, Gerard caught Fred's eye. "Thumbscrews!"

"Oooh!" the crowd gasped.

Fred gulped.

A lively discussion of torture in the eighteenth century ensued, amid trowels full of dirt and the continued screening for artifacts.

He didn't dare look up again. Gerard was watching his every move. He could feel it. Fred was sure Gerard would love to try the thumbscrews out on him. The crazy soldier no doubt knew exactly how to crush someone's thumbs and fingers in the simple vice.

Hunger chewed at his insides. He must have played pretend archaeologist long enough to take a break without rousing suspicion. Fred stood up and stretched, only to almost cry out in pain as the box slipped, digging into his leg.

It slipped again.

He lurched forward and grabbed it as it slid and scraped down his thigh.

"What's wrong with you, kid?"

Gerard didn't miss a trick.

"Leg cramp," Fred wheezed, holding the box against his thigh and limping away from the crowd. He continued about twenty metres, as far as he could get from Gerard, and collapsed on a low stone wall.

The box slid down his calf. He shook it out of his pant leg, quickly shoving it behind him. Had he been seen? Luckily, Gerard was busy enthusiastically demonstrating the thumbscrews to some of the awestricken volunteers.

Grace and Mai hurried over.

"Are you okay?" Mai's eyes were filled with concern.

He nodded.

"You don't look okay," she said. "What's wrong, muscle still cramped?"

He nodded again, but this time with a small smile. Nurse Mai's attention—he liked that.

"You probably need water. Have some of mine." She held out her insulated water bottle.

"Thanks." Fred grabbed it, his heart skipping a beat as his fingers brushed hers. He tilted his head back and guzzled a mouthful.

"I'm sick of this. Talk about boring—it's nothing like looking for fossils." Grace tugged off her Dalhousie baseball cap and rubbed the back of her hand against her forehead. "Besides, it's a gazillion degrees out here."

"What's going on, Fred?" Mai asked.

"Yeah, and it better be worth it." Grace flopped down on the ground beside him, stretching out her legs.

Fred stared up at the sky. He'd found the box. So it wouldn't be jinxing anything to talk about it now, would it? His problems were over. He could tell them. He wanted to.

"Fred!"

"Gimme a minute, Grace."

"We almost got arrested for you today," she griped. "You owe us."

"Owe you?" Fred said. "How many times did we almost get arrested for *you* just a few months ago?"

"Enough, you two!" Mai said. "Fred, we're your best friends. You can tell us anything." She reached over and gave his arm a squeeze.

Mai's slender hand on his arm made his mouth go dry. "Sorry I've been kind of mysterious. It's...well... complicated."

"It's you, Fred," Grace joked. "How complicated can it be?"

"See?" he protested. "You never take me seriously. That's why I didn't tell you in the first place."

"Sorry." She grinned. "I couldn't resist."

"You'll be taking that back," he said, gulping another swig of water.

"Wait. I need chocolate," Grace said. "Break out your stash."

"Don't mention chocolate," Fred groaned. "I'm starving, too."

"Well, where is it?" Grace asked.

"No stash."

Mai and Grace had identical shocked expressions on their faces. "No stash?" Mai said. "But you always have chocolate. Loads of chocolate. You don't go anywhere without it."

He squirmed, not willing to share *that* much of his story. "Didn't have time," he lied.

"Great, Fred," Grace complained. "*I* didn't bring anything to eat because *you* always do."

"Don't worry, I have food," Mai said. She zipped open a side compartment. Fred swore he'd never seen a backpack with so many pouches.

Grace rolled her eyes at him. *Ick*, she mouthed, pointing to Mai's pack.

Fred nodded, making a face. Anything Mai had brought hadn't come from the junk food section at the corner store, that was for sure.

"Voila!" Mai said. "High-fibre meal bars. I keep them for emergencies."

Fred unwrapped one and took an unenthusiastic bite. Nuts and birdseed weren't much of a substitute for chocolate, but his growling stomach wasn't so choosy.

Sighing and chomping off another bite, he settled back to tell his tale. "It all started over two hundred and fifty years ago at this very place..." He paused, lowering his voice. "With a stolen identity, a fortune in jewels, and *a murder*!"

Chapter 4

"MURDER?" MAI'S EYES GREW BIGGER than ever. "There was a murder?"

Several volunteers glanced their way.

"Not so loud," Fred hissed.

"Sorry!"

"Anyway," he continued, his voice barely a whisper now, "Claude Gagnon was my great, great, great, great, great, great...wait a sec—how many greats was that?"

Grace kicked his ankle.

"Okay, okay! Gagnon was my ancestor. And he lived right here, at the Fortress of Louisbourg."

Mai gasped. He had Grace's attention, too.

"So that thing you found, it was his?" Mai guessed.

He had them hooked now. "I'll get to that."

"What is it?" Grace asked. Her voice got higher. "The jewels? Let me see!"

"Shh!" Fred's heart hammered. He glanced up. Sure enough, Gerard was frowning at them from across the site. He'd heard something! This was a mistake. He should have waited. The box seemed to chastise him, too, its sharp corner digging into the back of his leg.

"Get my backpack," he said. "I've got to hide the box."

Grace stood up, but Gerard had already started in their direction.

"No time," she said.

"Quick, Mai, pass me your bag," he said.

"No, you'll mess it up. Use Grace's."

"Mai!"

"Oh, fine," she said, reluctantly handing over her bag.

He whipped open the pack, pulling out a handful of items and tossing them onto the ground. Grabbing the slim metal box behind him, he slid it between his legs and into Mai's open bag at his feet.

Gerard had already crossed half the distance toward them.

Fred stuffed Mai's things back in on top and tugged the zipper closed just as Gerard reached them. Had he seen the box? Grace jumped out in front of him.

"What are you three doing over here?" Gerard asked, peering around her and staring at the pack at Fred's feet.

"Taking a break," Fred said. He tried to sound casual. But what was the point? Gerard could probably hear his heart pounding.

"What's in the bag?" Gerard asked. He reached out as if to grab it.

"Nothing you didn't see already," Fred said, tucking Mai's bag between his legs and out of reach.

"You put something in there."

"Like what?"

"I don't know—something."

"What something?" Mai said. "You've been watching us the whole time."

"Yeah," Grace chimed in, her voice louder. "What have you got against kids anyway? Think we all steal or something?"

Gerard looked behind him. All the volunteers had stopped excavating and were watching them. The archaeologist was on her feet. "Is there a problem?" she called out.

"Uh, no, nothing," Gerard said. "Just checking on the boy."

"Is he okay?" The archaeologist started walking toward them.

"He's fine. Aren't you..." Gerard stared down at him. "What's your name, kid?"

"I'm not telling you."

"Listen here, you—"

"Everything all right?" the archaeologist asked. Grey hair jutted out in every direction from beneath the brim of a tattered Tilley hat. It was just like one Fred's grandfather used to wear. She smiled down at Fred with kind blue eyes.

"Yes, ma'am," he murmured.

"Very good," she said. "Did you all enjoy your experience here at the fortress today?"

"Oh yes," Mai said. "It was a lot of fun. I'm going to write a report for my class."

"That's marvellous," she said. "Be sure to send me a copy here at the fortress. I'd love to read it."

Mai blushed.

"What about you?" The archaeologist turned to Grace.

"Uh," Grace murmured. "Well, sort of. I, um, like fossil hunting better, though."

"I see," she smiled. "Well, you were all very well behaved. I didn't realize we were involving students as young as you in the program. I'll have to find out whose idea that was. Perhaps we can add to it next year."

Fred gulped. He hoped she didn't start asking questions too soon.

"I don't believe I have you on my list," she added. "Make sure you sign in so we can send you a follow-up questionnaire about your experience here."

"Ah, sure," Fred said. He stood up, passing the pack back to Mai.

Gerard's eyes narrowed, his head turning to follow the pack switching hands. The guy was downright creepy. Did he have X-ray vision or something?

Although Fred was nervous not having the box as close, it was a relief not to have the metal digging into his leg. They continued their work beside the archaeologist. Sifting slowly through the soil for broken pieces of old stuff was not exciting—at all! Finally, when they were done for the day, they helped her pack up, hoping that Gerard would give up and leave.

For a while, it seemed like they were never going to get rid of him. But eventually he growled something about being late for his shift at the gate and left. He turned around and glared at them one last time. Fred shivered. He was sure they hadn't seen the last of him.

They walked up the hill with the archaeologist, back toward the fortress. She was chatting away, telling them to be sure to seek her out if they had any questions, and that she was usually at the museum. She was so grateful for all their help, was going to write to their principal—blah, blah, blah. Fred was only thinking of one thing—finally being able to open the box.

It was a relief when the archaeologist turned up the lane to the museum. They continued into the reconstructed streets of the fortress. The scene was much different than when they had arrived in the quiet of the early morning. Tents had appeared, scattered along the quay, the main street that ran along the oceanfront. Re-enactors, many already in their period costumes, were busy setting up their sites.

Fred's leg was itchy and raw where the box had scratched it. Spots of blood had seeped through the front of his jeans. He needed a Band-Aid.

"C'mon, Dad probably set up the tents already," he said, turning right. "Yeah, here we are." Two shabby canvas tents were erected side by side, tucked in front of a couple of isolated buildings. They were at the edge of the reconstructed town area, a small guard lookout post beside them on the water side. *Will ghost soldiers of the past keep watch for us?* he wondered.

"Cool," Grace said. "It's like we're camping in the candy part of a lollipop. That road is the stick," she said, pointing to the quay and following the straight wall with her finger, then making a circle motion, mimicking the seawall that curved around them, the two buildings, and the guard post.

"And we're in the round lollipop," she finished, spinning around in their campsite.

"Lollipop?" Mai laughed.

"Well, I'm starving," Grace said. "Everything in my head comes out as food."

Fred peered into the tent closest to the wall. "My and Dad's stuff is in this one. You guys can stay in the other one. I'm going to change."

Fred closed the front flap of the tent. Finally, he was alone. Now he could examine the box. He yanked open the zipper on his pack. Then he remembered—the box was in Mai's bag.

Sighing, he pulled off his jeans and examined his leg. A few scratches ran down his upper thigh. He prodded the stinging injuries with his fingers. They weren't deep. He was surprised. It had felt like the box had been tunnelling to his leg bone.

He pulled out his clothes, looking for a clean T-shirt and pair of shorts. There wasn't much room to move around. His head brushed the slanted canvas roof. As he hauled his soot-covered shirt over his head, he almost fell over.

A large black duffle bag was taking up almost half the floor space. His dad's diving bag. He gave the bag a vicious kick. Why did he still have his diving gear? And why would he bring it here? Well, Fred had the box now, so it didn't matter anymore. But still—his dad had promised.

"Fred?"

"Coming, Mai." He stepped back into the sunlight. "Got your first aid kit?"

"Of course, why?"

"Need a Band-Aid...and my box."

"Band-Aid first." She gave him a gentle shove toward a rectangular opening in the wooden wall. "Sit down." It would have been a perfect place for a cannon, back when the fortress was operating. In fact, there were cannons in other identical openings in the wall closer to the main gate.

"What's the damage?" she asked.

He pulled back the cuff on his shorts.

Mai gasped. "Good grief!"

"It's not as bad as it looks." He grabbed her backpack from her before sitting down. "Can I?"

"Oh, go ahead," she mumbled, pulling things out of her first aid kit.

He scanned his surroundings to make sure no one else was around. Carefully, he lifted out the box. It was actually rectangular, not square. And a small black metal handle sat in the middle of the top. That must be how to open it. He gave the handle a tug. It didn't budge.

"Stop squirming!"

"Ouch!" Fred gritted his teeth at the sting of the peroxide.

"Don't be such a crybaby," Mai scolded.

He pulled the handle harder. Nothing. His fingers felt over the surface, searching for a latch or some other way to unlock the lid.

"It's stuck!" He stood up to get better leverage and yanked harder on the handle. It was sealed tight.

"Sit down, I'm not finished." Mai poked him.

Off balance, Fred stumbled. The box flew out of his hands, smacked into the wall, flipped over, and then landed on the gravel. He lurched forward and scooped it up, grabbed the handle and pulled.

"Open!" he yelled, giving it another forceful tug. He frowned.

"What's the matter?" Mai said.

"It's no use. It's sealed shut."

Chapter 5

"GEEZ, FRED," GRACE SAID, EMERGING from the girls' tent. "Yell a little louder, why don't you?"

Had he been loud? Clutching the box, he retreated into the hollowed-out section of the wall, expecting Gerard to come blazing around a corner any second.

"Stay still." Mai pounced at him and finished cleaning his cuts. "It's not too bad. I think you only need a bandage—no stitches."

A steady stream of re-enactors were making their way down the quay, laden with tents and supplies. Most were turning up side streets and heading to camp on the slopes around the King's Bastion. The rest were stopping along the way, picking sites along the seawall, closer to the main buildings.

Some sites were quite elaborate, with cooking areas and displays of activities like rope making, or different artifacts.

It did look pretty cool—like a living, moving picture from a history book.

Luckily, no one had set up tents anywhere near them. They were off the main track, so Fred hoped it would stay that way. There wasn't much extra room. He'd memorized the map and guide for the entire fortress. The two buildings behind them weren't furnished inside yet, so they were closed to the public. That's why he had suggested to his dad they set up their camp in this spot. Less traffic, hopefully.

"So, what's the scoop?" Grace asked, pointing to the box. "Are we rich?"

"*We?*" Fred said.

"Treasure hunters or fossil hunters, it doesn't matter," she said. "We split three ways."

"Yeah, right," he said. "Anyways, I've got a problem."

"What's the matter?" Grace asked.

"It won't open."

"Let me see." Grace held out her hand. "It's probably just stuck."

Reluctantly, Fred passed over the box.

Grace turned it around, tugging on the handle.

"Duh, you think I didn't do that already?" he said.

"Just checking." She smirked. "Sometimes you miss the obvious."

"Forget it. Give it back."

"Hold on, Freddo, I'm only kidding. Don't be so touchy." She sat cross-legged on the ground beside him, leaning her back against the thick wooden beams of the wall.

"I couldn't find a release latch or anything like that," he said.

She ran her fingers slowly over the edges. "Mai, give me one of those wipey things of yours."

Mai passed over a wet wipe and sat down beside her.

"There are some indentations here," she said, digging soot and dirt out with the wipe. "This looks like a keyhole."

Fred's heart sank. "But we don't have a key."

"Hang on," Grace said. She held the box closer to her face, squinting. "It's shaped like a keyhole, but it's all plugged up."

"With dirt?" Mai asked.

"I don't think so."

"What, then?" Fred edged closer.

I don't know." Grace rapped her knuckles on the top. "Something harder."

"A piece of rock?" Fred asked.

"Maybe..." Grace said.

"Give it here," Fred said. "If it's a rock, we can dig it out."

Grace passed the box back to him. "What are you going to use?"

"Where's your knife, Grace?" Fred asked.

She fished it out of her pack, opening the blade. "I think the blade's too big," she said. "But you can try it."

Fred tried to poke it in the keyhole. "You're right, it's too wide," he said, disappointment washing over him. Frustrated, he tried the other gadgets attached to the Swiss Army knife. Nothing worked.

"You need something longer," Mai said.

"Like what?" Fred asked.

"Try these tweezers from my kit."

He poked at the hole with the tweezers, but it was too

awkward to fit. Yanking the two sides apart, he broke the tweezers into two pieces.

"Hey!" Mai said.

"Sorry, I'll get you another set." He used the sharp, narrow tip to dig around the hole. There *was* a tiny piece of rock jammed in there. He popped it out. But the hole was still blocked. No matter how much he tried to clear it out, he couldn't.

"Another rock?" Grace asked.

"No." He tossed the scratched and mangled tweezers aside. "There's nothing *to* dig out. It's as deep as it goes. The hole is filled in. With metal, I think."

"Metal?" Grace sounded surprised.

"Yeah, and around the whole top and any other place there would have been a crack or anything…it's all been totally sealed up."

"That's weird," Mai said. "Who would do that?"

Fred stared off across the harbour. It made sense, he supposed. Maybe he would have done it, too. "Claude Gagnon."

"Your ancestor?" Grace asked.

He nodded.

"But why do that?" Mai reached over and ran the tip of her index finger around the edges of the box. "Then he wouldn't be able to open it either."

"I think he knew he'd never see it again," Fred said. "And wanted to protect what's inside."

"What happened to him?" Mai breathed.

What had it been like here over two hundred and fifty years ago? Had there been guns roaring overhead as the

British laid siege to the fortress? Had the thunder of cannon fire shaken the ground?

"He was murdered."

"No!" Mai gasped.

"How do you know?" Grace asked.

"My great-aunt Hughena had the old family Bible. When she died, Mom got it."

"What was in it? A treasure map or something?" Grace asked excitedly.

"No, nothing like that."

"What, then?" Mai asked.

"A letter, sort of."

"Oh. This is sounding like a long story," Grace said. "I'm starving! We should eat first. Besides, we've still got to figure out how to open that thing."

"What are we going to have?" Mai asked.

"Anything but those birdseed bars of yours."

"Oh, sure, Grace," Mai said. "They were good enough this afternoon."

"I need *real* food!" Grace said.

"Dad picked up stuff, I think. There were grocery bags in our tent." Fred started to get up but Mai waved him back down.

"We'll get it."

Fred rested on the low wall, his sore leg stretched out in front of him as Mai and Grace disappeared inside his tent.

Oh, crud! Had he left his underwear on the floor?

He sprang to his feet and was about to pull the flap back when he heard Mai and Grace talking inside. He stopped.

"Grace, look," Mai said.

"Can't you find the groceries?"

"Yeah, I did, but..."

"Well, come on then, I'm hungry."

"Wait."

"What's the matter?"

"Look at this," Mai whispered. "It fell out of the bag."

"What is it?"

"Grace, this slip says 'Sydney Mines Food Bank.'"

Oh no!

Fred closed his eyes. What was he going to do now? Run? Where would he go? But he couldn't face Mai, not now. This was his stupid father's fault. If he'd sold his diving gear like he'd promised, they would have had some money and—

"Hey, *Freddo*. Long time no see."

This couldn't be happening.

Fred slowly opened his eyes.

"Hello, Jeeter."

Chapter 6

JEETER LAUGHED, SLIDING A LARGE duffle bag off his shoulder. "Good to see you too, Freddo." He reached over and punched him lightly in the arm.

The jab stung, but Fred refused to flinch. "Didn't think I'd ever see you again," he said, flatly. Who had told him they were here? Mai? The thought was like a punch to the gut. No, she wouldn't have done that. It must've been Grace.

Things were going from worse to worst.

Jeeter shrugged. "Well, better get used to it. Dad and I are moving here."

"What?"

"He got a two-year assignment at the Tar Ponds project." Jeeter leapt to the top of the wall, dangling his legs over the side.

EEEEEKKKKK!

The shrill scream shot through the air like a laser. A flash of purple was all Fred saw of Grace as she ran past him, almost knocking him into the wall.

"You're moving here, for real?" Grace yelped.

Jeeter grinned down from his perch. "I know. Cool, eh?" He grabbed Grace's outstretched hand and hauled her up beside him. "Miss me?"

Grace's face flushed poppy red. "Don't get a swelled head," she said. "But it won't suck having you around…I guess."

Jeeter tilted his head back and laughed. "Who could get a swelled head around you?"

Fred's stomach felt like he'd swallowed a flushing toilet, and it was stuck, spinning crazily in circles. Jeeter sat up on the wall like some prince on a throne, soaking it all in. What was it about the guy? This annoying, know-it-all jock whose mission seemed to be to ruin Fred's life.

Well, maybe that was an exaggeration. But Fred knew Mai had had a crush on Jeeter before the summer. And with Jeeter back, strutting around, there was no way she'd be interested in Fred. Even Grace's excitement at Jeeter showing up ticked Fred off. Grace and Mai were *his* friends, not Jeeter's.

It seemed like everything about Jeeter was the opposite of Fred—he was tall, muscular, and un-clutzy. Did he live at the gym? Fred even felt like his brain shrank when Jeeter was around, like he was just some stupid kid.

Fred tensed as the flap on his tent moved. Mai emerged, the groceries clutched tightly in her arms. Her head was bent over the bag and her hair had fallen forward, hiding her face.

She can't even look at me. Shame burned through him. He couldn't stand it. He mumbled out loud, "Be back in a minute," and dashed around the tent. He staggered through the open gate between the two unoccupied buildings, slamming it behind him.

Blood rushed to his head. He felt dizzy. Dropping the metal box on the ground, he doubled over, pressing his hands to his knees and sucking in a deep breath. What was he going to do? The thought of facing Mai's pity was unbearable.

He sank down on his haunches and leaned back against the wooden siding of the empty building. The gate remained closed. No one had followed him. Were they talking about him right now? Probably. No wonder. *The food bank!* He could kill his dad right now.

The worst of it was that no one had had to find out about this. His family would have lots of money once he sold the treasure.

Fred scooped up the black box, brushing off the dust. His fingers scraped against the sharp edges. There had to be a way to get it open. Holding it to his ear, he gave it a shake. Something was inside, sliding from side to side. But there was no rattle.

The jewels must be wrapped up, protected. Yeah. That made sense. He examined the sealed seams of the box again. What could he use to open it? Here, in the middle of the fortress? Nothing sprung to mind.

Standing up, he tucked the box into the back of his shorts, pulling his shirt out over. Luckily his shorts fit better than his jeans, and the box was snug against his skin. He wished he didn't have to go back to the tent site. Well, he could wait a bit. Maybe some miracle would happen and Jeeter would disappear.

What if they just went home? He had the box. There was no reason to stay. He could ask his dad. But…what if the jewels weren't in the box? If they weren't, he'd need to return to the excavation site. And if he left the fortress, that wouldn't be possible. No, he couldn't risk it. He had to get the box open, and then they could go home. For now, he'd have to suffer.

The courtyard between the two buildings was partially finished. Some gardens had been planted, with green sprouting up through the earth in even rows. But the other half of the area was still just mounds of dirt and gravel. Fred looked into one of the windows of the vacant building. There was nothing inside. It would be cool when they got it finished, he thought.

A hand clamped down on his shoulder. "What do you think you're doing?"

Fred jumped, swinging around to get caught in the glare of the mean, black eyes of Gerard the crazy soldier. *Not again!* he thought.

"Well?"

"Nothing." Fred wiggled free of Gerard's grip and stumbled two steps back.

"This isn't open to the public. You're not allowed in here." Gerard's gaze darted around the courtyard, as if looking for some sign of criminal activity.

"Sorry."

"Blind, are ya?" Gerard spat into the dirt.

"What?"

"I said, 'Are you blind?'"

"No."

"So you saw the *No Trespassing* sign," Gerard accused, thrusting the end of his rifle at the painted sign on the gate. A vein was pulsing over his right eye.

"Uhh...not really."

"Out!"

Fred edged past him without protest, careful to avoid the end of his rifle. The secluded, fenced-in yard wasn't the best place to be alone with a crazy man, he realized. What were the odds he'd run into him twice in a few hours? Then he remembered Gerard's coworker saying something about his over-the-top behaviour.

"Move it," Gerard prodded.

"Were you...spying on me?" Fred guessed.

Gerard froze. "Beg your pardon?" he blustered. Now he was the one to take two steps back.

"I should get my dad," Fred said.

Gerard glanced nervously over his shoulder. "We'll just make this a warning," he muttered. Not even bothering to wait for Fred to leave, he spun around and strode off.

Maybe that'll keep him off my back, Fred thought. What was the guy's problem, anyway? It's not as if it were wartime, like back in the 1700s. Louisbourg was only a park now. But something told him it was all very real to Gerard. Vowing to keep an eye out for the wacked-out re-enactor, Fred reluctantly left the quietness of the courtyard.

The idea of returning to the campsite and Jeeter-the-jock wasn't appealing, to say the least. So instead of turning right and following the curve of the seawall, he veered left, onto the quay. Maybe he could find something to open his box.

The grassy slopes of the King's Bastion were dotted with more tents than before. The weekend pretend soldiers, their backs bent with the heavy packs of tents and supplies, continued on the route to their right, up the hill. It seemed everyone wanted to be in the centre of the action, none coming as far as their edge of the reconstructed town limits.

Fine with me, he mused. The fewer witnesses to his constant humiliations, the better. Santier House was to the left, the last structure on the quay. He strolled along the main street, past Morin House.

A red door surrounded by stone in Le Billard's foundation caught his eye. It was more the size of a window, with a small, square hole in the middle. The hole was trimmed in wood, like a framed picture. Two strips of metal shaped like swords spread from the hinges on the left across the door. They almost touched the large rusted lock on the right. Fred pressed his face into the opening. It wasn't even big enough for his head to fit through. Blocking out the only source of light, Fred could see nothing. The smell of damp earth and the whiff of something rotten filled his nostrils. Not an appealing prison, he thought, pulling his head back and examining the outside lock. He wondered what offences had been committed by its past prisoners.

The crowds were thickening farther ahead at the centre of the quay, by the Frédéric Gate. The smells of roasted meat and fresh-baked bread drifted from the restaurants. His stomach rumbled. Thinking of the lint that filled his pockets instead of money, he turned back toward the campsite where food was waiting. Hunger won over embarrassment—for now.

A figure darted behind the tents as he approached. "Dad?" he called, sure he recognized the trademark black jeans and matching T-shirt. The figure didn't pause.

"Dad?" he repeated, louder.

Curious, he stopped in front of the vacant buildings where he'd had the run-in with Gerard. The gate was still swinging shut. He stepped closer, holding it ajar. Murmured voices came from inside the courtyard. Fred peered around the gate. His father was talking to a man he didn't recognize. He was huge! Dressed in a loose white shirt and short pants, with long socks and wooden shoes, he had to be a re-enactor.

Fred was about to say something, when the man pointed his finger in his dad's face. "We had a deal."

"We still do."

"You said you'd found it," the stranger said.

"It's complicated."

"Well, uncomplicate it!"

"Relax," his father said. "I'll figure something out."

"You'd better. I'm counting on this."

"Give me 'til tomorrow night. I've got a friend on the *Invictum*. It's just taking a bit of time. Don't worry, I'll find you."

"I'm on the hill. With this getup, I blend in with the rest of the crazies up there." The man kicked at the dirt. "These shoes are ridiculous!"

"Best I could do," his father said with a shrug. "I gotta go."

Fred carefully let the gate close and hurried around the back of the building. He watched from the corner as the man strode off down the quay. His dad walked in the same direction, but circled around on the quay side of their campsite. He could hear Grace and Mai's cheery greetings. Fred closed his eyes and leaned his forehead against the side of the building.

His head was spinning. Like he didn't have enough to worry about already. What trouble had his dad gotten into?

Chapter 7

FRED SUCKED IN A DEEP breath and rounded the water side of the tent site. The firepit was burning brightly. Mai was laughing and busily opening cans and dumping the contents into a metal pot. Jeeter was sitting between Mai and Grace, looking like he owned the place. They all lifted their heads in his direction. All eyes but Mai's met his. He felt like he was barging into someone's house uninvited.

"Nice of you to join us," Jeeter said. "Where did you take off to?"

"Uh, bathroom," he blurted.

"I guess when you gotta go, you gotta go," Jeeter smirked.

"Did you get it open?" Grace asked. "I'm dying to see. Remember, we split three ways!"

"Get what open?" Jeeter asked.

"Nothing!" Fred hissed, glancing at the tent. "Not now Grace, okay?"

Grace looked confused but nodded, her gaze switching from Fred to the tent and back again. *I'll have to explain that,* Fred guessed. Although he didn't know how he would. How do you explain that you don't trust your own father?

Mai was quiet, sitting cross-legged by the fire, and hiding behind her hair curtain again. Was she ever going to look at him? And he couldn't go into the tent. His father was in there and he really didn't want to get into the whole thing about the diving gear—not where everyone could hear, anyway.

"What's the matter?" Grace demanded.

"Nothing, why?" Fred asked.

Grace stood in front of him with her hands on her hips. "Don't pretend. Something's up. You're acting even weirder than usual!"

"Forget it."

She leaned close to his ear, as if not to be overheard. "You don't have to split four ways, if that's what you're worried about. I'll give Jeeter some of my share."

He rolled his eyes. "Geez, Grace."

"Fine, I'm just saying." She returned to her seat between Mai and Jeeter.

Fred picked a spot away from the fire. He sat down gingerly and stretched out his legs. From its hiding place, the box dug into his back. It was like an angry cat, scratching him for attention. *Be patient, I'm working on it!*

Grace was yacking her head off to Jeeter about the fossil project underway on the Point Aconi beach. He was asking about her dad. Mai stirred the contents of the pot as it sat on a grill above the flames. He wished she'd look up. She was concentrating on the pot like it was the most important thing in the world. He closed his eyes and leaned back against the beams of the seawall.

Grace and Jeeter's chatter faded to a dull buzz. Visions of giant rubies and emeralds swam behind Fred's lids. He imagined himself floating over the fortress. Something here would help him get the box open, he knew it. The details of the maps and sketches of the buildings he'd memorized were suspended around him, like a 3-D movie. It was a *fortress,* after all, with weapons.

An idea about how to open his box was just out of his reach. He squinted, as if that would make it come into focus. He pictured the entrance gate. To the right was the bakery. No, not there…but beside it was—

KKLANGG!!!

A muffled curse came from the guys' tent. Fred's eyes sprang open. The canvas wall facing the water flapped madly. What was his dad doing in there? Then, just as quickly, he realized he'd rather not know. Some crazy scheme to make money, Fred suspected, thinking of the shady character his dad had met earlier.

"Hungry?" Mai asked softly.

She held a steaming bowl of stew out toward him. Fred's heart flipped as he met her gaze. Her lower lip was quivering. "Are you all right?" he asked.

"I didn't know," she sniffled. A teardrop hung from her lower eyelash. "I'm so sorry."

He thought for a moment of pretending he didn't know what she was talking about. But what was the point?

"It's fine," he muttered. Why was he feeling bad for Mai because she was upset? He was the one that was poor! *Girls.*

"I want to help."

She didn't know the half of it. Some things no one could help with. "It's fine," he repeated, "really."

"Fred, I mean it."

Behind Mai, Grace and Jeeter were staring at them. Grace was probably dying to hear what they were whispering about. She was so nosy.

He lowered his voice even more, motioning Mai closer. "As soon as I get this box open, there won't be anything to worry about."

"I don't want a share. You keep it."

"Grace is nuts, don't listen to her. There are no shares. It's all for Mom anyway." Rats! He hadn't meant to say that.

"Your mom?"

Scenes of the past two months flashed in his head. He still couldn't believe how fast his life had changed. He remembered going to Grace's birthday party with Mai at the beginning of the summer. It had almost seemed like a date. Everything had been perfect. Now it was the end of August, and it was as if it had all happened to someone else. In a way, it had. He felt different now.

"I won't tell anyone," Mai said, her voice hushed.

"It's a long story," he said. "I—"

"Are you guys going to eat or what?" Grace said, waving them toward the fire.

"Yeah," Fred answered. "Sure. But you better hide those cans. It's supposed to be all real cooking from the old ages, remember? I don't think canned stew was on the menu back then."

Mai hesitated. Fred could tell she wanted to talk more. He edged closer to the fire. After a second, she followed. They settled around the firepit. There was an awkward silence for a few minutes, but Grace couldn't seem to stand it.

"Jeeter, you missed a good one today. You should have seen this crazy soldier guy," she murmured between mouthfuls. "Totally crackers! He thinks he's back in the 1700s somewhere, waiting for the British invasion."

"Figures," he grinned. "First day and you're already in trouble."

"Wasn't me," Grace said. "Freddo's the trouble magnet now."

"I saw him again," Fred said. "That fortress soldier—he followed me."

"*What*?" Grace said.

"He's crazy all right," he added. "I think he's after, you know..." He shifted slightly, feeling the weight of the box against his skin.

"What?" Jeeter asked.

"Fred's box," Grace said.

"Grace!"

"What? He'll find out eventually, Freddo." She shrugged, scraping out the last bit of stew from her bowl. "When we get it open."

"What's in it?" Jeeter asked.

"Treasure," Grace added with relish.

Fred's father emerged from the tent. "Treasure?"

Oh no! Fred desperately tried to think of something to say. "A story we heard today," he rasped, his throat bone dry. He coughed.

His father studied each of them, his eyes finally resting on Fred. "Story, huh?"

Fred doubled over, now in the throws of a coughing fit. The box poked painfully into his lower back. It didn't seem very happy, either.

"Not holding out on your dear old dad, are you, son?" His father flashed a wide grin, slapping Fred between his shoulder blades. "Treasure's right up my alley."

Chapter 8

"YOU KNOW ABOUT TREASURE?" GRACE leaned forward. "Tell us."

Fred's father didn't need further encouragement. Mai and Grace made room for him in the circle and Mai handed him a bowl of stew.

"I've travelled the world," he said. There was a gleam in his eye. Or was it the flickering reflection of the fire? "And seen more treasure than you could ever dream about."

Grace and Mai exchanged puzzled looks.

"But..." Grace said.

Fred could read their minds. Why were they getting meals at the food bank? Why weren't they living in a big mansion? "He's leaving out the important part," he said. "It wasn't *his* treasure."

"It was." His father scowled. "I got swindled!"

Fred rolled his eyes. Not this story again. “Dad, you were a hired hand, remember?”

“Fred!” Mai gasped. She looked horrified. She’d probably never had so much as an argument with her parents, let alone talked back to them.

“No, no, it’s okay,” his father said, holding up a hand. “He’s right. Or at least the judge thought the same thing.” He stared off at the water. “But that’s not how it was. We were partners.”

“What kind of treasure?” Grace asked.

“Gold. So much gold, it took us a week to get it all up. Millions!”

“Get it up from where?” Jeeter asked.

His father smiled. “The bottom of the Bermuda Triangle.”

There was a collective gasp. All eyes were fixed on Fred’s father. He had them.

“The Bermuda Triangle? For real?” Jeeter looked impressed.

Fred’s father nodded. “And everything they say is true. It doesn’t give up its secrets easily.”

Fred shook his head. He knew what came next. Heck, he could probably tell the story even better than his father could after all these years. “Why don’t we check out the rest of the fortress?” he suggested lamely.

Grace shot him an “Are you crazy?” look. “Wander around this boring old fort? We’ve got all weekend to do that. I want to hear about the treasure.”

“Me too,” Mai added. She looked apologetically at Fred.

“Fine,” Fred grumbled.

"It was an accident," his father continued, "us finding her. Maybe she wanted to be discovered, finally, *L'Herminie*."

His father poked the fire with a stick. Flames licked high, sparks drifting down around them. Fred knew he was taking his time, loving the fresh audience.

"You were the first to find the boat? Oops, I mean find *her*?" Mai breathed.

"This part of *L'Herminie*, yes. The main part of the wreck had been discovered years before. But she'd broken up and been scattered all over the coral reefs. Cannons and such had been recovered...but never gold."

"How did you find it?" Grace asked.

His father paused, as if trying to recall the details. Fred bit the side of his cheek, holding back the "Gimme a break!" that was on the tip of his tongue.

"The sea was flat as a table that morning. Not a cloud in the sky. The site we'd been searching hadn't delivered at all. A few cannon balls, some knives and odd bits, nothing like we'd hoped. We had done an entire grid of the bottom, too. Took our time."

A group of re-enactors were strolling by on the quay. They stopped, looking over at everyone gathered around the fire. "Evening," one said.

Fred's father waved casually, but didn't return the verbal greeting. He made no effort to stand up. The group murmured amongst themselves and resumed their walk. One glanced back their way. They seemed to sense that they weren't welcome.

His father poked the fire again, sending a fresh spray of sparks into the darkening sky. "We packed it in and were heading to port. I was on deck, cleaning the dive gear. The da—"

Fred coughed, aware his father was about to swear.

His father looked up.

Fred shook his head.

"Oh, ah…the *darn* tank fell over and started rolling down the deck. I bent over to grab it…"

Grace leaned forward. "What happened then?"

"WHAM!" his father roared, smacking his two hands together.

Grace jerked backward. Her water bottle toppled off her lap and spilled into the dirt. Mai squealed and grabbed Jeeter. Even Fred, who knew it had been coming, twitched.

"White wall! A rogue wave came outta nowhere. Swamped the boat. Almost sank us."

"Oh my gosh!" Mai's brown eyes glowed in the firelight. "Was anyone hurt?"

Fred's father pointed to a scar on his forearm. "Used up one of my nine lives that day."

Mai put her hand over her mouth.

"Cool scar," Jeeter said.

His father grunted. "Lost most of the equipment. Electronics were fried. We drifted for hours." He settled back from the fire, his voice lowered to normal. "Ended up hung up on some coral."

His eyes were half-closed and his speech had slowed. He always got like this. Fred figured his father was reliving every detail in his head. It reminded him of movies where characters talked about the fish that got away. L'Herminie's gold was his dad's fish.

"Were there any, you know, sharks or stuff like that around?" Mai asked.

His father nodded and pressed his lips together. "There are always sharks. But if you don't bother them, they won't bother you...mostly." He scooped a heaping spoonful of stew from his bowl.

Mai shuddered. "None around here, though, are there?"

His father smiled. "You'd be surprised what's swimming around our little ocean—sharks included."

"What? I'm never going swimming again!" Mai vowed, gazing fearfully at the harbour.

"Sharks, schmarks! What about the treasure?" Grace chimed in.

"Ha, got you hooked, eh?" Fred's father winked. "So, where was I? Oh, yes, the coral...Anyway, the boat wasn't leaking, so we figured there was no need to panic. Since we lost the tanks, I patched myself up so I wouldn't bleed in the water and decided to do a little snorkelling while Nip worked on the radio."

"Nip?" Jeeter asked.

"Dad's boss," Fred said.

"*Partner,*" Fred's father corrected. "It was a sweet dive—the reef was pristine. A school of sergeant majors were keeping me company, but a barracuda or something must've spooked 'em. They scattered and...there it was."

"The treasure?" Grace said.

"You bet. Laid across the sea floor like a picnic on a blanket."

"Wow!" Grace said. "That would be awesome."

"There's nothing like the weight of a gold doubloon in your hand," Fred's father said, closing his fingers and rubbing them together.

"You didn't get to keep *any* of it?" Mai asked.

"Nip was the one who always took care of the paperwork." His closed hand tightened into a fist. "I guess you never really know someone until there's a king's ransom at stake."

No one spoke. Their glazed eyes danced eerily in the firelight. Fred figured their minds were dancing as well, imagining what having that kind of money would be like. He used to wonder, too. But he didn't have to anymore. The box was tucked safely under his shirt. Fred had done what his father never could. He had his own treasure now and no one was going to take it away.

Chapter 9

THE QUAY HAD GONE QUIET. The fortress was closed and the re-enactors seemed to have settled down at their sites. The place was deserted.

Fred's father had disappeared, mumbling something about a bathroom. Mai and Grace were helping Jeeter pitch his tent on the other side of the vacant buildings. "Unless you'd rather I bunked with you?" he'd joked to Fred.

Alone, finally, Fred pulled the box from under his shirt. He was so certain the jewels that his ancestor, Claude Gagnon, had mentioned in his letter were in it. But his father's story of betrayal was still fresh in his mind. What would someone do for money? Anything.

Who knew for sure what had happened in those final hours? Only Claude, and he sure wasn't talking—he had spent over two hundred and fifty years in his grave.

How much were the jewels worth? It would be enough—it had to be enough.

He clutched the black box. Whatever was going to happen with this treasure, Fred would be in charge. His father messed everything up. That's why he wasn't going to tell him about it. Had that Nip guy really cheated him? Fred had always thought it was wishful thinking on his dad's part. Nothing ever seemed to work out like his dad promised.

Who knew what his dad was even up to now? That big guy he had been talking to hadn't seemed very friendly. And why did his dad have his dive gear? Fred gazed out at the sea. Its surface was smooth, like his dad's story of the Bermuda Triangle that day he said he'd found the treasure. There were tons of wrecks out in the Louisbourg harbour and even more along the coast at Little Lorraine and Chameau Rock and Scatterie Island. Was one of them loaded with treasure—his dad's chance to catch that big fish?

Fred knew a bunch of the French ships had gone down in one night in the harbour, during the British invasion in 1758. *L'Entreprenant* had been shot at by the British and caught fire. Two other French ships in the harbour had drifted close enough that they also fell victim to *L'Entreprenant*'s hungry flames. Gagnon had talked about that night in his letters, too. Had the ships been loaded with treasure…escaping before the British could steal it?

Tall ships dotted the calm harbour now. Echoes of voices from the hill and firelight flickering from the re-enactors' campfires made it easier to imagine the scene long ago. All that was missing was the thunder of the cannons.

KAABOOMMM!

What the...? Fred ducked, holding the box over his head. He glanced around wildly, hearing shouts from the bastion. Were the British invading again?

"Cool or what?" Grace whooped, leaping into view.

"Cool?" Fred could hear his voice shake.

"Not scared are you, Freddo?" Grace joked. "It's part of the fun. Mai said they'd be shooting cannons after hours and other stuff for us all weekend, you know, after the fortress closes."

"Oh, right. Awesome."

Grace squinted at him, as if trying to tell if he had been scared or really knew all along. "Uh-huh."

Get a grip! All that thinking about Gagnon had him a little nuts. "Where's Mai?"

"Oh...I kind of smashed the hammer on Jeeter's thumb while we were putting up the tent. Mai's fixing him."

Fred frowned, peering around the edge of the tent. Only a small sliver of Jeeter's tent was visible. *What's Mai doing over there?* he wondered.

"Why don't you just ask her out already?" Grace said.

Fred gulped, feeling heat creep up his neck. "What are you talking about?"

"Geez, Fred, you've liked Mai ever since we were kids." Grace kicked at the glowing remains of the fire.

"How do you—how did you—I don't—" he blustered.

"Don't bother trying to deny it. It's written all over your tomato-red face."

He stayed silent. It wasn't like he could have talked anyway. It felt like he'd swallowed a box full of chalk. *Grace knows?*

"Don't let your head pop off," Grace said.

"I'm not!"

Grace pursed her lips. "Want me to ask her for you?"

Fred felt like he was being yanked into a wormhole. "No!" he managed to croak. "You can't."

Grace laughed. "You're freaking out. Chill, Freddo. I won't tell."

He managed to suck in a breath at that. Life might not be ending after all.

"You really think that's full of jewels?" Grace said, pointing toward the box.

Fred blinked. Man, it was hard to figure out girls. Their heads zigzagged all over the place. In a split second, she switched from threatening to tell the biggest secret of his life, to the thing that was going to save his life: his treasure.

"Well?"

"Yeah."

"Guess you won't have to worry about, you know…food…anymore, huh?"

WHAM! A punch to the gut. He'd forgotten all about the food bank disaster. "Guess not…"

"What about your dad's dive shop?" Grace said. "I mean, none of us are rich. Well, except maybe Mai. But you always had…stuff."

"Dad lost the shop. It closed a couple of weeks ago."

"Oh."

Fred closed his eyes. "And then Mom couldn't go back to the bakery. They hired someone else. Not that it mattered.

She couldn't have climbed up and down those stairs all day anymore, so..." He drifted off. It had happened overnight almost. Lots of food and an allowance...then suddenly bare cupboards. No chocolate milk. No favourite cereal. No choco stash.

"What happened to your mom?"

"Long story."

"Sorry," Grace mumbled. "Why didn't you call us? We could have—"

"It doesn't matter now," he butted in. "I'm going to fix everything. We'll even get a new house, maybe—a big one. A big, flat one with no stairs."

Grace stared at him for a second, then grinned. "Yeah, you better get that choco stash back, too. I can't take Mai's disgusting granola crap much longer."

Fred laughed. "I know, it's *gross.*"

"What's gross?" Mai asked.

Grace looked over at Fred and they both laughed even harder.

"What?"

"Nothing," Grace said. "Inside joke."

Fred tossed and turned in his sleeping bag. He had safely hidden the box. He looked over at his dad's empty sleeping bag for the hundredth time. It was after midnight and he'd been gone since supper. Where was he?

He could hear a low rumble. It sounded like snoring. Was it Mai? No way, he decided immediately. Mai didn't snore. It had to be Grace.

CRRUNCH!

Someone was outside the tent!

Fred held his breath. Maybe it was Grace or Mai, going to the bathroom or something.

He heard the sound of a match being struck. A faint smell of cigarette smoke drifted in through the tent opening. Rolling over, he peered through the sliver of the tent entrance. His father was standing perfectly still, facing the water. The moon was perched round as a beach ball over his head.

"Better get it tomorrow," his father said softly.

Fred pulled his sleeping bag up past his chin and closed his eyes just as his dad entered the tent. He tried to breathe slowly, as if he was asleep. Cold droplets hit his face from above. He concentrated on not moving. Pretending. He didn't know why. He could feel his father standing over him.

Fred still didn't budge. Eventually, his father continued to the other side of the tent. Fred dared open one eye and saw him getting changed.

SQUELCH!

The clothes sounded heavy as they hit the floor.

He remained perfectly still until he heard his father's breathing eventually slow. He was finally asleep. Fred licked his lips. The dripped liquid was…salty. Sea water? He quietly reached his hand over, feeling for the pile of clothes. They were soaking wet.

Fred lay there, wide awake as the fortress slept. What was his father doing out in the ocean in the middle of the night?

Chapter 10

"NO WAY AM I WEARING this."

"You have to, Grace, or you can't stay," Fred snapped. She was impossible. "We have to wear stuff like they did back then for this re-enactment thing. That's the deal when they let you camp here."

Mai reached over and smoothed out the front of Grace's apron. "It's kind of pretty," she said, "a nicer blue than this dark one." She bunched the skirt of her own dress in her hand.

"At least your outfits don't scratch like a blanket of fleas," Fred said, pulling the short wool pants away from his skin. "And it's hot as a sauna in these freakin' things."

"A dress!" Grace ranted. "No one said anything about a stupid dress." She stomped around the campsite, sending puffs of dust into the air.

Fred twisted in his white shirt. The sleeves were like wings. He should have been able to take off into the sky. But they were too tight under the arms. "Man, this sucks," he huffed, giving up the struggle. He flopped onto one of the tree stumps they had for seats.

"So what are we supposed to do, go around in bare feet?" Grace stuck out her foot. "Or can we wear our sneakers?" she asked as she tugged down on the dress. It only went to her ankles.

"You're gonna love this," Fred said. He dumped out the remaining contents of the canvas sack. Three pairs of wooden clogs fell into the dirt.

Grace and Mai gaped at the shoes like they were slithering snakes. "You're kidding, right?" Grace said.

"Nope," Fred said.

"That's it," Grace said. "Stick me in this dumb dress, fine. But I'm not walking around with trees on my feet."

Mai slipped her foot into one of the clogs. "Ewww!" she yelped, kicking it off. "There's something in there."

Fred picked it up and shook it out.

Plop!

A grey-brown *something* fell to the ground. They all leaned over it.

"What *is* that?" Grace asked.

Fred squatted on his haunches and poked it with a stick. It wasn't grass or dirt, or an old sock. *Uh-oh.* He scooped it up and chucked it over the seawall before Mai or Grace could get a closer look.

"Just a bunch of old moss and dirt." *Attached to a dead mouse!* He figured he'd better leave that part out.

"It didn't feel like moss to me," Mai said, viciously scrubbing her foot with a wet wipe.

"It looked kind of like a—"

"Grace, shut it!" Fred hissed through gritted teeth.

"What?" Mai asked suspiciously.

"Nothing," Fred said. But he made sure to check the other shoes while Mai scrubbed out the inside of the one she'd kicked off.

Early risers were already walking through the fortress grounds. That was the sucky part of the encampment, Fred realized. Even though it had gotten him into the fortress, there were way too many people around. How was he going to get the box open without anyone else seeing?

"Okay, so we're in these weird old clothes. Now what?" Grace asked.

"Explore the fortress," Fred said. "I have to find something to open this box."

"Where's your dad?" Mai asked, passing around more of her granola goop. "He sure is busy here, isn't he?"

"Don't know," Fred said. Dad and his dive gear had been missing when he woke up that morning. Streaks of red from the rising sun had licked angrily across the sky like a raging grass fire. He'd shivered as an old saying popped into his head: *Red sky at night, sailor's delight. Red sky in the morning, sailors take warning.*

He glanced out toward the water now. Mist hung low over the harbour, hiding its secrets. A tall ship drifted into view, silent and slow as a ghost ship. His attention was caught by a sign posted on the shore:

I bet whatever Dad's doing, he didn't get permission from anyone. Fred's head was buzzing with possibilities, each worse than the last. No one scuba dives in the middle of the night if they're on the up and up.

"Here, you must be hungry."

Fred examined the granola bar Mai was trying to put in his hand. Birdseed and varnish. He wasn't *that* hungry. "Uhh, I'll save it for later. Not hungry."

"Hmmm, too bad. Here, Grace, I *know* you didn't eat anything yet."

Grace grimaced and took the offering.

"So, what's the plan for today, anyway?" Mai asked.

Fred grinned. "Only one plan—get my treasure open."

"Treasure?" a gruff voice said.

Oh no, not crazy Gerard again! Thankful that the box was still hidden in his tent, Fred turned around. He had to tilt his head back to look up at the guy. Ice-cold grey eyes stared down at him from the middle of a face fenced in by a unibrow, long sideburns, and goatee.

The giant from last night!

Chapter 11

"WHAT?" FRED ASKED. HE BLINKED up at the re-enactor his dad had argued with the previous night. One of his eyes drooped lower than the other, the lid half closed. Maybe he usually wore an eye patch—like some super-sized pirate. With the guy already wearing a puffy shirt and cut-off pants, it wasn't hard to imagine. He just needed a parrot on his shoulder.

"I heard you say 'treasure.'" The man stepped closer.

Fred could smell him—sweat and burnt bacon. "N-no... what?" He gulped. "Oh, that! We were just—"

"Making up a game," Mai said.

The giant's eyebrow rose to the middle of his forehead. "Really? What kind of game?" He nudged past Fred and peered into the tent opening.

"W-what are you doing?" Fred asked.

"Friend of your dad's," he said. "Thought I'd stop by to say hello." He lifted back a tent flap and stepped closer. "Where is he?"

"He's not here."

"So I see." The man continued looking into the tent. Finally, he turned back to Mai, Fred, and Grace. "Tell me more about this game of yours."

It didn't sound like a request. Fred's brain was in overdrive. All he could think about was protecting the box. It took all his willpower to stay put and not run into the tent and grab it.

"We thought it would make the encampment more fun," Mai said.

"How's that?"

"Um, you know…pretend there's a treasure…and, uh… explore around to find it." She tugged on her hair. If she didn't stop, she'd pull out a chunk.

"Yeah, you know, just kid stuff," Grace chimed in.

"Kid stuff," the giant repeated. He glanced back at their tents.

Fred felt like he could read his mind. The giant wanted to search them. Fred couldn't let him do that. He wouldn't.

"What's going on?"

Jeeter strolled toward their site from the quay. He was taller and more muscular than Fred remembered from earlier in the summer. What was he doing, popping muscle pills?

The giant turned to face Jeeter. "Who would you be?"

"I'm me," Jeeter retorted. "Who are you?"

The giant surveyed them, one by one. Then he seemed to make a decision. His grim face changed. "Ha, ha," he chuckled, "enjoy your *treasure* game, kids."

Fred, Jeeter, Mai, and Grace stood in a semi-circle and glared. Fred wasn't interested in pretending to be friendly.

"Yes, well," the giant continued in his Mr.-Nice-Guy voice. "I'm *sure* I'll see you around." He winked at Fred and started walking away. "Oh, tell your dad I said hello," he called back over his shoulder.

Fred felt the strength drain from his legs. He leaned against the seawall.

"Freddo, my man," Jeeter said with a low whistle. "This is some mess you're in."

Fred's eyes followed the giant as he walked along the quay toward the front gate. He stopped, leaned against the corner of the LaGrange House, and stared back at them. The giant grinned and lifted a hand in greeting.

Mess was an understatement!

Huddled in Fred's tent, the four friends were almost sitting on top of each other.

"Do you think he's gone?" Mai asked.

"Don't know," Fred said. "But if he thinks we're hiding something, I don't think he's going to go far."

Grace fidgeted, pulling at her dress. "We can't stay here all day."

"I know," Fred said.

Mai was tugging her hair again. Grace was right. They couldn't stay cooped up in here all day. He ran through the map of the fortress in his head. If they could make it away from the tent undetected, they'd be home free. There were plenty of places to hide on the fortress grounds.

"Okay," Fred said. "I've got an idea." On his hands and knees, he poked his head out from under the rear of the tent. The coast seemed clear. "Come out," he said. Mai, Grace, and then Jeeter crawled behind him out from under the canvas.

"Now what?" Grace asked. "If we go out on that quay thingy, we'll be spotted for sure."

They stood, squished together. Mai was pressed against his side. Her smooth hair brushed against his chin. He breathed in the sweet scent, wishing he could freeze time and stay in this moment.

"Yo, Fred," Grace snapped. "What now?"

So much for the moment.

With another quick survey to make sure they weren't being watched, he dashed across to the gate between the two empty buildings. He waved the others on and they scurried to join him.

He led them through the gate into the enclosure with the garden. He'd remembered right—there was another gate at the back of the garden. He unhooked the latch and stuck his head out. Still clear.

Crouched behind the building, Fred peered around the corner at the end of the quay. A few tourists were walking up from the ruins. But there was no sign of the giant or crazy Gerard.

"We'll go straight up to the museum and then around the back of the fortress to the bastion," he said. "That circles the outside of the town. If the giant still has our campsite under surveillance from the same spot, we should miss him."

"So, who is he?" Mai asked. "I mean, he knows your dad, right? Why are we hiding from him? Other than because he's gigantic and scary looking?"

"Ummm," Fred stalled. What could he say, really? It was only a hunch, after all. He didn't know for *sure* his dad had hooked up with a criminal.

"Fred," Mai said. "You have to tell us—what's going on?"

"Yeah," Grace said. "Seriously, it's bad enough we're trying to stay away from Gerard the psycho soldier, and now we've got *another* stalker?"

Fred studied the faces of his two best friends. They looked a bit...scared. Even Grace. What would they think about his dad's meeting with the giant the night before? Would they find the conversation as suspicious as he did? But they'd already found out so much about Fred's life—too much. Besides, he could be totally off base. "I don't know," he said, "just a feeling."

"A feeling?" Jeeter asked. "That's it? Now you're psychic?"

"Psychic? Awesome. Tell me my future," Grace said. She held her finger to her forehead. "Wait, I'm getting something. Yeah...I see bags of money. No...make that a room full of money...and jewels..."

"I told you, no sharing."

"Funny Freddo," Grace said. "Three ways—I'm not kidding."

Fred stormed ahead on the dirt path that bordered the left side of town, up toward the museum. Grace got on his nerves sometimes. As if he was going to share. The money from the jewels was for something really important. Life-or-death important. He just hoped it was enough.

Chapter 12

THE DIRT FROM THE DRY road churned in mini dust devils as they walked up the low hill. Tiny specks of rock bit Fred's face. He squinted up at the sky. Thick clouds were racing by on fast-forward. A gust of wind from the white-capped sea whistled across the ruins on his left.

"Ouch! I got dirt in my eye!" Grace said.

"Here, let me see," Mai offered. "I've got a clean cloth. Jeeter, come stand beside us and block the wind, okay?"

Wind-blocker Jeeter. Another thing he was better at, just because he was taller. Mai, Grace, and Jeeter huddled together. Fred turned sideways with his back to the trio, the wind, and the sea. The rebuilt town of the Fortress of Louisbourg was laid out below him. The bastion with its tower and multitude of chimneys stood guard to his left, up the steep slope, a dozen soldiers marching toward its front gate.

Somewhere in the maze of houses, military quarters, and shops below was a way to open his box. To save his family with his ancestor's treasure. The box! He'd left it well hidden beneath his sleeping bag, thinking it was safe there in case they got frisked or worse by Gerard. Now, doubt filled him. He shouldn't have let it out of his sight.

Of course Jeeter chose that second to come over. "So, what's the plan again, Freddo?"

"I have to go back to the tent for a second. Be right back." Fred was already heading back down toward their site.

"Where are you going?" Mai called. "Fred, wait."

"You guys stay here—I'll only be a minute."

That's when he saw him. Charging up from the town. Headed straight for them. The giant! They hadn't fooled him after all. His instinct to flee took over. He whirled around. "Run!" he cried.

"Run?" Mai said. "What's wrong?"

Fred shoved her in front of him. "Giant!" he yelled.

"Eeep!" Mai squealed. She grabbed Grace's sleeve and the four of them scurried up the slope. Well, as fast as they could with chiselled tree stumps on their feet.

Fred frantically scoured the landscape. Maybe they could hide in the tall clumps of grass and wildflowers on their right. Were the plants tall enough to hide them if they scooched down?

Grace stumbled. "Stupid cloggy crap shoes!" she cried.

"The museum," Jeeter said, veering left.

Everyone was panicked. They were like a pack of herbivores being chased by a Tyrannosaurus rex. They tripped up the stone steps after him, the four of them tumbling through the entrance together, a mass of arms and legs. Someone's clog went flying and sailed through the air.

Thunk!

Klunk!

Plunk!

It bounced like a skipping rock into the middle of the floor. Fred looked down at his feet. Of course it was his. He unwrapped his arm from around Jeeter's leg and pulled a wad of Grace's hair, which was still attached to her head, from his mouth.

The few nearby tourists had all turned from the displays and were staring. Glass cases lined the walls of the large open room, filled with unearthed artifacts. In the centre was a miniature model of the fortress, fully rebuilt and including the ruins. His shoe had skidded underneath it.

Fred kept his eyes glued to his shoe as he hobbled toward it like a pirate with a peg leg. *Klap. Klap. Klap.* His steps with his wooden-clad foot echoed off the high ceiling. He slid his socked foot into the wooden shoe. As he turned around, the unfriendly giant barged through the entry.

He loomed menacingly, blocking out the light. As strange as Fred and his friends' clumsy entrance must have been, this new distraction seemed to trump it. In unison, all eyes in the room fixated on him.

And he was a bewildering sight. With his giant stature, pirate-like dress and unsmiling face, he looked like a larger-than-life cartoon villain. Shadows accentuated his scowl as he glared at Fred.

"My goodness, whatever is going on here?"

Fred turned to meet the confused gaze of the archaeologist they'd met on the dig the day before.

"My avid young archaeologists," she said. "Causing another ruckus, I see?" Her kind eyes crinkled at the corners.

"Sorry," Fred mumbled. "I tripped."

Her smile widened as she noticed his footwear. "Well, no wonder, with those things on your feet. Come for that visit?"

Fred stared at her blankly. Visit?

"Yes, that's right," Mai said. She'd scrambled to her feet and was smoothing her tousled hair.

"Excellent."

More light seemed to suddenly fill the room and Fred glanced back toward the doorway. The giant had vanished. What if he went back to their tents? Fred felt sick. He had to get back there. "Um, actually, maybe we could come back later. I just remembered—"

"Nonsense," the archaeologist said. "It's no trouble at all. Come along, I'll give you a personal tour."

Fred looked helplessly back at Mai, Grace, and Jeeter. Grace shrugged. Well, how long could it take? It was only one room, after all.

How wrong he was. Case by case, they worked their way around the exhibit. Each buckle, halberd top, ice creeper, door handle and belt hook was described in excruciating and boring detail. The handcuff and thumbscrew display barely even caught his attention. And Mai was making it ten times worse with a question every thirty seconds.

They moved on to another case. Mai's lips parted. Fred tapped her ankle with the pointy end of his shoe.

"Ouch," she whispered, shooting him a dagger look.

"Stop with the questions. We haven't got all day!" he hissed back.

"I can't help it. They just pop out."

"Pop them back in." He manoeuvred in front of her so he was closest to the archaeologist.

"And here we are, the last case," the woman announced with a flourish.

Finally! Fred pretended to be interested, leaning obediently forward to look in the case. His breath caught. Inside were two boxes just like his. And a bunch of wrought-iron keys.

"What are these?" he asked, tapping the case.

"Oops, don't touch the glass," she chastised. "You mean the boxes?"

"Yes, do they open?"

"You are a peculiar young man," she said, shaking her head. "The torture devices you barely blink at. But metal boxes you're excited about?"

"What was inside them?" Fred continued. "Can we take one out? Do those keys fit?"

"Whoa! Let me think. I'd have to check the records, but I don't recall any notations that there were objects found inside. I'm not quite sure if the keys even belong to these particular boxes. All of these artifacts were likely found at different locations across the grounds."

Fred stared intently at the boxes, trying to memorize every detail. They really did look identical, except the keyholes weren't filled in. "Could I hold one?"

"Absolutely not, I'm sorry. That is not permitted."

He bit back disappointment. "What about the records? Would they say if the keys came with these boxes and where they were found?"

She looked at him curiously. "Why on earth would you want to know that?"

"I, uh…really like…boxes," he said, feeling a flush creeping into his cheeks.

"Is that right?" She didn't look convinced.

"I thought…" He racked his brain. "Maybe I could write about them for school or something. You know, part of our report."

She brightened and shot him a huge smile. "What a fine idea. Anything that gets a student interested is worth a little effort. Even if it's metal boxes. Give me a moment."

She bustled over to a door marked *Do Not Enter—Employees Only.* She took a key from her pocket, unlocked it, and slipped inside.

"Geez, Fred, enough with this lame place already," Grace groaned. "I'm going outside."

"Me too," Jeeter added, following Grace toward the door.

"What are you up to, Freddo?" Mai asked.

"One of these keys might fit my box."

"But you heard her. You can't take them out of the case."

Fred could feel the excitement rushing through him. His fingers twitched, ready to do his bidding. "We'll see about that."

Chapter 13

"*WE'LL SEE ABOUT THAT*?" Mai yanked his arm, pulling him around to face her. "What's that supposed to mean?"

Reluctantly, he dragged his eyes from the keys in the case. "Just what I said."

"You can't mean...are you saying you'd *steal* them?" Shocked round eyes stared at him like he was some alien creature.

He winced. It sounded really bad when she said it out loud. "Of course not."

"Whew! You had me worried there for a second." Mai relaxed her hold.

"I'm going to return them. So it's only borrowing, not stealing."

"*What?*"

"Shh, here she comes," Fred said.

The archaeologist re-emerged and carefully closed the door behind her, then locked it. "Well, good news and bad," she said. "There are records, just not here at the museum."

"Oh," Fred said.

"Not to worry," she added. "They were moved over to the records room at the King's Bastion. I'll pop over this afternoon and have a look, shall I?"

"If it's not too much trouble, uh, Professor..."

"Just Molly. And it's no trouble at all." She grinned and patted his shoulder. "I'm thrilled you're so interested. And to write a report for your school? Warms my heart!"

Fred shifted uncomfortably. "Uh, thanks."

"That's what I'm here for." She waved a casual hand toward the displays. "I should get your school information. If you're doing a report, the least I can do is let them know what a help you all were. Since we don't pay volunteers, maybe you'll get some extra credit from your teacher, especially working on your summer holiday."

"I think I wrote it down..." Fred trailed off. Good grief, they'd made up doing a report, and now she wanted to contact his school? Classes didn't even start for a week. No teacher who knew him would ever believe he was doing a report voluntarily. Mai, yes. Him, definitely not.

"No." Molly eyed him expectantly.

Mai had turned pale. Fred was sure she was going to crack if he didn't get her out of there right away.

"I'll give it to you when we come back," Fred offered. He'd put in a fake school and phone number if he had to. "When you get the information on the boxes and keys?"

"Lovely," she chirped. Her gaze drifted to a family of tourists wandering past the displays. "Excuse me, won't you? Duty calls." She hurried off to the opposite end of the room.

"C'mon, let's go," Fred said.

They walked down the stone steps and paused on the dirt road. No one was in sight.

The wind had vanished completely. Ominous charcoal clouds hung low and the air was still. It was kind of weird. Like the sky was holding its breath. And where were Grace and Jeeter?

"Psst!"

"What?" Mai asked.

"Wasn't me," Fred replied.

"You and I are the only ones here."

"Psst, is he gone?"

Fred peered across the dirt road at a thick patch of high grass. "Grace?"

"Yeah, is he gone?"

"It's just me and Mai."

The grass moved and Jeeter and Grace emerged. "Finally," Grace said. She stood on the dirt road and shook out her skirt. "I swear a grasshopper climbed up this dumb dress. That wouldn't happen if I had pants."

"Stop complaining. You'd have been in shorts anyways," Fred said. "What happened?"

"The giant came back again. We barely had time to dive into the weeds," Jeeter said.

At least Molly's longer-than-long tour had had one benefit. Giant guy had given up, for now. Fred had to get his box.

"I gotta go back to the tent."

Ignoring him, Mai breezed past Fred and walked over to Jeeter. "You've got grass in your hair," she said.

"I do?" Jeeter lifted his hand toward his head.

"I'll get it." Mai stood on her tiptoes and placed her hand on Jeeter's shoulder. She reached up and pulled strands of grass free, waving them in front of his face. "See?" she laughed.

Jeeter smiled down at her. "Thanks."

Fred swallowed. "I, uh, gotta go."

"We're coming too," Grace said. "Safety in numbers, I say."

"She's right," Jeeter said. "Whatever that guy is after, we have to stick together. Maybe we should look for your dad and find out what's going on."

"Grow some gills and maybe you can," Fred muttered.

Jeeter raised his eyebrows. "What are you talking about, Freddo? Did you say *gills*?"

"Never mind." He started walking down the hill.

"What are you doing?" Grace asked. "We can't go that way. It's all in the open—we'll be sitting ducks!"

Fred stopped. Much as he hated to admit it, she was right. The road back down the hill was flanked by gravel and short grass. Absolutely no hiding places. They needed cover. Giant guy could come back any second. What about the King's Bastion at the top of the hill? Lots of people and cover, but it was in the wrong direction.

The large patch of meadow directly in front of them would hide them for most of the way to the edge of the town. Then there were lots of places to hide as they made their way back to their campsite on the quay. "Okay, I guess you're right."

"What was that?" Grace smirked, her hands on her hips. "Could you say that again? I didn't hear you."

"Oh, stuff it," Fred grumbled. He waded into the tall grass. Well, not really grass. More like a maze of tall brown stalks with fuzzy, dull-white balls on top, like dandelions. But it did the trick. When he crouched down a bit, the stalks were over his head. Crickets trilled as Fred, Mai, Grace, and Jeeter began to snake through the weeds.

They inched forward, popping up every few minutes to check for the giant. It seemed like he really had given up on them. Maybe he had already gotten what he wanted from the tent, Fred thought. No! He'd hidden it well. No one would find it.

But then, who would even be looking for it? No one knew he had it, right? Maybe he was overreacting. He didn't even know this giant guy. He was probably just being paranoid.

Something flew into his mouth. "*Pllfff!*" Fred spat. A swarm of no-see-ums had come out of nowhere and enveloped them in a cloud. The miniature flying pests were everywhere at once. In their mouths. Up their noses. In their ears. They were under attack! Gagging and spitting, they pushed forward through the last of the meadow, their arms waving crazily over their heads at the receding cloud of bugs.

Pieces of the fuzzy flowers were stuck to their clothes. Fred kicked off the wooden clogs and dumped them out, bits of dirt and plants scattering on the ground. Grace and Jeeter's complaints were a faded drone in the background.

He looked up to find Mai staring at him. He recognized that look. Disappointment. She probably thought he was becoming a total criminal. But there was nothing he could do about it right now. Borrowing a bunch of old keys was nothing, really. The box was too important.

On the lookout for the giant and crazy Gerard, they zigzagged through the streets, from one building and group of tourists to the next. Halfway down the main street, they paused in an arched doorway. The smell of baking apples from inside the building taunted their noses and stomachs.

"That smells so good," Grace said. "Let's go in."

"I'm hungry, too," Mai said, stepping inside. "Come on."

Fred's fists clenched inside his empty pockets. How much did it cost? What difference did it make? He had no money. His stomach rumbled. "You guys go in, I'll be back."

Jeeter wrapped his arm around his shoulder and edged him inside. "Don't worry, Freddo, this one's on me."

Fred pulled away. "I'm not hungry."

"Freddy, is that you?"

Fred froze. He stared into the dark gloom of the restaurant's interior. A thin figure approached him. She walked slowly, her shoulders slightly bent. Her eyes were rimmed with dark circles—brown eyes that used to twinkle but were now flat and dull.

"Mom?"

Chapter 14

"WHAT ARE YOU DOING HERE, Mom?" Fred said. "You should be home."

"I'm fine," she replied, grinning weakly. "Marjorie called me. One of the waitresses quit and she knew we needed—"

"Does Dad know about this?" Fred could feel heat burning in his ears. This was his dad's fault.

His mother shook her head. "I only found out last night. You two were already here." She placed a hand on his arm.

He tried not to wince. Her fingers were ice cold, even through the fabric of his shirt. "Quit."

"Sweetheart, I can't do that."

"He should be the one getting a job, not you!"

"That's enough," his mother replied. Her lips pressed into a thin line. "Now come in and have something to eat."

"Mom—"

"Sit," she ordered.

He sat—at an unoccupied table against the back right wall. Even though seeing his mom had thrown him for a loop, thoughts of the giant were not far away. Choosing the seat against the wall, he faced outward. Never leave your back exposed to your enemies. He knew that from the movies. Good advice.

His mother turned to Mai and Grace, her voice soft and sweet. "What a delight seeing you two. It's been a while."

Mai looked like she was trying to swallow something that wouldn't go down. Her eyes were extra bright as her gaze slipped to Fred's. It was no longer filled with disappointment. Pity had taken its place. He liked that even less.

"Nice to see you too, Mrs. D." Grace's voice sounded scratchy as she slumped onto the bench seat beside Fred.

"I don't believe I know you," his mother said to Jeeter. "Are you one of Freddy's school friends?"

"Uh, yeah, I guess," Jeeter said, scooting to the far end of the table.

Fred watched his mother as she chatted to his friends, recommending food choices. She was so…delicate. A strong wind would whip her around like a leaf. It was as if she was being erased, a little at a time. No wonder Mai and Grace were reacting this way—they hadn't seen her all summer. She'd lost so much weight. She was—

"Freddy, did you hear me?"

He snapped back to the present. "What?"

"What did you want to eat?" His mother was looking at him expectantly.

"I, uh..." he said, scrambling. *What's she doing? She knows I don't have any money!*

"It's okay," she added, as if reading his mind. "I'll take care of it. What do you want?"

"You pick," he said. She finished their order, which didn't take long. A menu from the 1700s wasn't full of choices. She took another order in French from a family of tourists at the next table, and then disappeared into the kitchen, and Mai excused herself to go to the washroom. Fred's mind wandered, churning with confetti pieces of worried thoughts.

Their order took awhile. The restaurant was busy. Finally, his mother returned with a large wooden tray laden down with food and drinks. Halfway to the table, the tray wobbled slightly. She was going to drop it! Fred leapt up and grabbed it before it slid from his mother's trembling hands.

"That'll teach me to carry a lazy man's load," she joked. It might have been funny if her voice hadn't been trembling, too.

Mai rushed in and plopped into her seat just as they began passing out the food. "Sorry, there was a line-up," she said, blushing.

Fred held the tray while his mom passed out glasses, a large pewter pitcher of water, and the dishes of food—bread and cheese to Mai, stew to Jeeter and Grace, leaving one dish and mug remaining.

"An apple tart?" Fred gaped.

His mom grinned, the hint of a twinkle returning to her eyes. "Why not dessert first? In fact, that's my new motto—

always eat dessert first! Your meat pie will be ready in a minute. And here's a hot chocolate. I know it's warm out, so excuse the hot. I figured the chocolate part would make up for that."

"Thanks, Mom." He grabbed the large spoon and dug in. The mouthful of sweet apples and thick syrup melted in his mouth. "Mmm," he groaned, washing it down with a swig of chocolatey heaven and wiping his chin on the large, white cloth napkin.

"Um, Mrs. D?" Mai said. "How am I supposed to cut my cheese with this?" She held up her large metal spoon.

"Sorry, dear," his mom said, "that's part of the authentic 1700s experience. You'll figure it out, I'm sure."

His mom started clearing the table across from them. Sunlight streamed through the white-paned window. She leaned over and unlatched it, pulling both halves open. A breeze blew through, rustling the strings of her bonnet. She lifted her face to the sunlight and smiled, closing her eyes.

Fred swallowed the sudden lump in his throat. Framed in flickers of sunlight and shadow, his mom looked just like before—before his world had flipped on its head. Before the normal parts of summer—beaches, camping, and picnics—had been replaced with doctors, hospital visits, and tests.

"This is not very practical," Mai grumbled. Digging with the dull end of the spoon, she was breaking off uneven pieces of cheese from the bigger cubes.

"Suck it up, Mai," Grace said. "It's not going to taste any different if it's not in perfectly even slices."

"Maybe not to you," Mai said.

Fred also inhaled the tart and spicy meat pie that followed. With a full stomach, his brain was back in overdrive. He had to get back to the tent and his legs twitched, anxious to get going. But as usual, Mai was the last to finish, dainty as she nibbled the small bits of cheese.

He stared around the silent table. Everyone was deliberately not looking at him. Grace was examining the small metal jug she'd picked up off the table like it was the most interesting fossil she'd ever uncovered. Jeeter was staring at the plastered log wall and Mai was playing with the cutlery and twirling her hair. He let out a deep breath, the sweet apples turning sour in his stomach.

"The cancer's back," he said.

Mai lifted her stricken eyes to meet his. "Why didn't you tell me?"

He couldn't explain why he hadn't called. How could he talk about the jumbled emotions and thoughts mashed together in his head when he didn't understand them himself?

"She got really sick at the beginning of the summer—pneumonia. She wasn't getting better, so they did some tests."

The darkness of the restaurant's interior and Fred's own thoughts began closing in on him. Feeling the sudden need for fresh air, he jumped up and strode out into the sunlight.

And ran smack into the giant.

Chapter 15

IT WAS LIKE SLAMMING INTO a fridge.

"Whoa, there." The giant grabbed his arm. "What's your hurry?"

Fred was stunned. The giant's steely eyes had all the warmth of a dead fish. *I'm not being paranoid!* Fred thought. *Something is definitely up with this guy.*

"Shark's son, right?"

"Shark?"

"Sorry, I mean Pete."

Fred didn't respond, wiggling out of the giant's grip.

"Excuse me," his mom said, wrapping her arm around Fred and at the same time drawing him away, closer to her side. "You know my son?"

The giant turned his attention to Fred's mom. A huge grin spread across his face. "No, ma'am. I'm a friend of his dad's. Name's Lester." He held out a meaty paw. "Pleased to meet you."

Her tiny delicate hand disappeared in his. "How do you know my husband?"

"We…worked together."

His mother continued to stare up at the man's face. Clearly, she was waiting for more. So was Fred. *Who is this guy, really?* The man glanced around, avoiding his mother's eyes. He didn't seem anxious to elaborate.

His mother's body tensed and Fred's friends gathered around him—a united front ready for whatever the giant had to throw their way. Images of old battles probably fought on this very spot hundreds of years ago popped into his head. Maybe those ghosts were on his side, too—ancient buccaneers with weapons drawn.

The giant shuffled his feet, obviously uncomfortable under Fred's mother's gaze. "Nice to meet you," he muttered, turning abruptly and walking off. His long legs took him around the next corner in only a few strides.

The air felt lighter. The sun brighter. Fred let out the breath he'd been holding. Another close call. Fred had the creeping suspicion that their next giant encounter would not be so easy.

"That was odd," his mother said, shaking her head. "Anyway, I have to get back to work. You kids have a great day." Her eyes found Fred's. "And *try* to stay out of trouble?"

"Don't worry, Mrs. D., we'll make sure he behaves," Grace said.

"Mmm-hmmm, I'm sure." His mother disappeared inside, swallowed by the shadows.

Fred moved sideways from the door to allow a group of tourists with sunburns and sweaty faces to enter the restaurant. One of them had a square black camera bag looped over his shoulder. It reminded Fred of his own black box. His steps quickened as he headed down the quay and in the direction of their tents.

The quay was clogged with people—weekend re-enactors, tourists, and fortress soldiers in army dress, all gathered in front of the Frédéric Gate. A man stood in the middle dressed in cut-off pants, a white shirt like Fred's, and a blue wool vest. His head hung low and he was flanked by two soldiers. His wrists were encased in handcuffs.

"*Voleur*?" Grace asked. "What does that mean—that wooden sign around his neck?"

"Thief," Fred said. The only break in the crowd was around the soldiers and the prisoner. He'd have to cut right in front of them. Anyone could be watching from the crowd. He'd have to wait it out.

"What are they going to do with him?" Mai asked. Her arm pressed against Fred's as they were squeezed by the crowd.

"I don't know." Fred saw himself in the prisoner's place, in handcuffs, being dragged off to face a criminal's fate. Even though he'd claimed the box was his, belonged to his family, part of him knew the difference. His dad chasing treasure on the open ocean was one thing, where finders were keepers. But here in a government-owned fortress? Well, that was something else.

"Hey, you guys," Jeeter said. "If you're staying here, I'm going to check out some of the other buildings. Meet you back at the tent in a few, okay?" He didn't offer for anyone to come with him and disappeared into the crowd.

Fred glanced over at Le Billard, the tavern. The padlocked red door with the tiny opening at the bottom. He recalled peering inside it the day before. What would it be like to be locked away in that dark hole that stank of rotting cabbages? He shuddered.

Another fortress employee stepped in front of the prisoner, facing the crowd, and unrolled a scroll. He was dressed differently—buckled shoes, a long coat, and a black, three-sided hat perched on a ponytailed wig. He scowled at the prisoner and began reading in a loud booming voice, first in French, then English.

"This man is a thief," he said. "Stealing bread from the King's bakery—a serious crime. The sentence from the court is branding and banishment from the town."

The prisoner looked suitably ashamed. The crowd cheered.

"Please, have mercy," the prisoner begged. "I was trying to feed my family."

"Is there anyone among you who seeks clemency for this criminal?"

A young girl close to the front raised her hand. "Let him go," she pleaded.

"Oh, good grief," Grace said. "It's not like they're going to really whip the guy—he works here."

"Don't be such a downer," Mai said. "Go with it. It's all part of the fun. Everyone knows nothing's really going to happen." She leaned closer to Fred and whispered in his ear, "Right?"

Distracted by the feel of her sweet breath on his neck, Fred didn't answer right away.

"Right?" she repeated.

"Huh? Oh yeah, it's all part of the act." *As long as psycho soldier Gerard's not in charge.* As if on cue, a tourist moved and there was Gerard. Their eyes met. Fred knew he was thinking the same thing. Did Gerard still have the thumbscrews found in the dig the day before?

"Very well," the officer droned. "Mercy for the prisoner." He turned to the prisoner and unlocked the cuffs. "Take heed, monsieur," he said. "Next time you will not be so fortunate."

The crowd clapped and started to disperse. The contingent of soldiers lined up and began marching back up toward the King's Bastion, their steps timed with the beat of the drummer. The man who'd read from the scroll was talking to a family of tourists next to Fred and Mai.

"Would he really have been granted a pardon back then?" a tourist asked.

The officer shook his head. "*Mais, non.* Definitely not. He would have been branded on his face or shoulder with a 'V' from a hot poker as a *voleur*, a thief. Then he would have been banished from the town forever."

"Were there worse punishments?" asked the tourist.

The officer nodded. "Oh yes, indeed. On one documented occasion, a man and woman who conspired to commit murder were sentenced to the wheel."

"The wheel?"

Fred leaned closer.

"Yes, the criminals were each strapped to a large wheel, with arms and legs stretched, and then tortured. The executioner beat them to death, breaking every bone in their bodies."

The tourists gasped. So did Mai. Fred had heard enough. At least if he was caught, no physical punishment would be involved. He wiggled and jostled through the milling crowd, his eyes focused on their tents. The sun shone brightly. The threatening clouds had vanished. Something moved behind the canvas. He quickened to a jog, imagining the giant ransacking the place.

"Hey, wait up," Mai protested. "What's the rush?"

"There's someone in my tent!"

Chapter 16

HE ROUNDED THE CURVE OF the seawall. The shadow moved again. Someone was definitely inside his tent.

"I see it!" Mai rasped. "You don't think that Lester guy would trespass in broad daylight, do you?"

Fred definitely did. He reached out to pull open the entrance flap, just as the intruder pushed it open from the inside.

"About time you kids showed up," his father said, stepping out into the sunlight. He grinned at them, his dark hair shiny and wet. "Where have you been? Having fun?"

"Fun?" Anger coursed through Fred like surging lava. Rather than the stalking giant, it was his mother that flashed in his mind. "Did you know Mom's working here?"

His father's eyebrows shot up, shock clearly showing on his face. "*What?* She's supposed to be resting."

"Yeah, well, Aunt Marjorie got her on at the restaurant. Mom says we need the money." Accusation dripped from each word.

A frown replaced the shocked expression. "I told her not to worry—I'm taking care of things."

Yeah, sure you are. Just like you took care of everything else. "How?"

"It's...complicated," his father said.

"Complicated? Complicated like how you got our groceries at the food bank?" Fred was shaking.

"Son, I told you, it's a temporary situation. I've got it under control."

"No you don't! You were supposed to sell your dive gear—but I saw it in the tent."

His father gripped Fred's shoulders and stared intently into his eyes. "I know you're angry. But I'll have good news very soon. You have to trust me. Can you do that?"

Trust. Fred wished he could. But years of failed promises had built a towering wall that was impossible to climb, and trust lay somewhere on the other side. "I can't—"

"Try. Just try for me, okay?" His father gave his shoulders a squeeze.

Fred shrugged out of his father's grasp. He couldn't say yes.

His father sighed and turned away. "Sit tight, I'm going to talk with your mother."

He was gone before Fred could ask him about Lester and what he was doing here. Although he was pretty sure the answer would be more of the same—that his dad couldn't explain and for Fred to trust him.

Fred ducked into his tent and away from the stares of his friends. He felt wetness on his face and wiped his eyes with his sleeve, surveying the crowded tent. Everything seemed to be undisturbed. Pulling aside his sleeping bag, he lifted the flat rock recessed in the ground. He reached down into the hole he'd dug beneath it.

His hiding place was empty.

The box was gone!

No. No. No! "It has to be here!" He burrowed under his clothes strewn over the tent floor, his father's sleeping bag, the duffle bags, the food, until it was all piled in a jumbled heap.

Nothing.

His legs flopped like unsnapped rubber bands and he collapsed back on the pile. *What am I going to do now?*

"Are you okay?" Mai peeked in through the tent flap. "It sounded like a stampede of wild animals in here." Her wide eyes took in the mountain pile in the middle of the floor and Fred collapsed on top.

He didn't answer. His heart was racing and tripping over itself.

"Fred?"

"It's gone," he croaked.

Grace poked her head in next. "Fred, are you okay?" She stepped in beside Mai.

"No," Fred said. He closed his eyes, picturing his dad standing in front of him. Shorts. Tucked-in shirt. No place to hide anything. "The giant stole my box."

"He must have had it when we saw him at the restaurant!"

Grace said. "If he'd just stolen it, why would he come looking for you?"

"It won't open, remember?" Fred said. He pictured the giant's puffy shirt—lots of room to hide his box. He stood up, his head clearing as his mind worked out what he needed to do. "He'd be looking for a way to get it open. And it's got a keyhole. Maybe he thinks I have the key."

"Isn't he missing the obvious?" Grace said to Mai.

"Umm," Mai murmured. She didn't say anything else, instead picking up a towel and folding it. She placed it neatly on the pile of clothes.

"What's obvious?" Fred asked.

"Your dad," Grace said. "He was just here. Do you think maybe...?"

"He didn't take it with him. He had no place to hide it."

Grace gave him one of her "You-are-so-stunned" looks. "He could have put it somewhere *else*, couldn't he?"

"No. I already searched in here."

"Maybe you missed it?" Mai said. She swept her arm at the mess. "If we clean up, we might find—"

"No point," Grace said. "Why would he hide it in here? He'd figure Fred would search everywhere. He'd put it somewhere else. That's what I'd do, anyway." She poked at the pile, causing an avalanche of clothes and dishes. A tin mug rolled across the floor. "But you still don't know exactly what's in this box thing, do you? How can you be sure it's even valuable?"

Fred checked outside the tent to make sure there were no eavesdroppers. Then he reached inside his waistband, pulling out a zip-lock bag with a bundle of yellowed, folded pieces of paper inside. "Because it's all in here," he said. Opening the bag and gently unfolding the aged parchments and his translated notes, he smoothed the pages carefully against his shirt.

"What's that?" Mai asked, leaning close.

"A letter. Well, sort of a journal, really. From my ancestor, Claude Gagnon. He was the sole survivor of the treasure ship, *Le Chameau*."

Grace sucked in a breath. "Treasure ship?"

"Yeah, and it's real," Fred said. "I mean it *was* real. I Googled it. It was wrecked off Louisbourg during a storm in 1725. They said there were no survivors—over three hundred lives lost. And there was *tons* of treasure on board."

"Wow, Freddo, you might really be on to something this time," Grace said. Her eyes gleamed and she slapped him on the shoulder. "A real treasure ship."

"Yes, and I've got to get my box back before Lester finds a way to open it!"

"Maybe there's something in the letter that can help?" Mai said.

"Not in the pages I found." Fred tapped the paper lightly. "Which are all in French, by the way. I had to use a French-English dictionary to translate it. It took forever!"

"Why didn't you just ask your mother?" Grace asked, looking puzzled. "She's bilingual, isn't she?"

Fred pressed his lips together. "She had more important things on her mind."

Grace's cheeks flushed. "Oh, right."

"Anyway," Fred said. "The pages tell all about that night, the night of the shipwreck...and everything afterward."

Mai and Grace looked at him expectantly. He had them.

"Well, don't keep us in suspense," Mai said. "What happened?"

Fred motioned for them to follow him as he side-stepped around them and out into the sunlight. He scanned the nearby faces. All were strangers. The coast was clear—for now.

Voices carried across the quay. Tall ships drifted in the harbour. Waves lapped the shoreline. Once again he had that sensation, as if he'd been transported back to the 1700s. It felt weird, like he was zigzagging between the present and the past.

"C'mon," Grace said. "Let's hear about this treasure."

He plunked down in the vacant cannon slot in the seawall. Grace and Mai sat on the ground, cross-legged in front of him. Mai tucked her skirt around her knees, a lock of her hair coming loose and falling across her face. She glanced up at him and their eyes locked. His fingers twitched as he had the sudden urge to reach down and tuck her hair back in place.

"Ahem!" Grace muttered.

Pulling his eyes from Mai's, Fred examined the papers. He knew the story so well. He fingered the aged parchment.

He'd spent so many hours with the words, translating them, reliving them. Maybe that's why he felt so connected to this place. The words were part of him now.

"There had been a full moon," Fred began. "The calmest night of the voyage. We had no idea what lay in wait for us. *Le diable.* The devil."

Chapter 17

"THE DEVIL?" MAI SAID SOFTLY, she and Grace leaning forward in unison.

Fred nodded. Feeling a breeze graze the back of his neck, his eyes were instinctively drawn to the sea. One of the tall ships eased by, members of its crew hanging from the rigging. The wind filled and billowed the untied sails with a series of loud snaps. Barked orders had the hands scurrying. The ship swayed in the white-capped waves.

Was it like that on *Le Chameau*? Fred imagined he could feel the deck tilt beneath his feet as he returned to his tale. He glanced down at the papers to find his spot. He continued with the story, in Claude's own words.

I had snuck up on deck as I often did late at night, my only opportunity to breathe in the fresh air and walk about freely. Monsieur Fornac was there, as usual, clutching his satchel to his chest. The man never slept.

From Claude's description in other pages he'd read, Fred could picture the round, bald man with the big mustache, always with a sheen of sweat on his forehead and darting, panicked eyes as clearly as if he was standing beside him. He continued:

I had been ordered to remain out of sight, to not draw attention to myself. I was not supposed to be there, you see, a lad of ten travelling on his own. But it was suffocating below decks, and the rocking waves caused my insides to churn. If I'd not had some respite, I would have gone mad.

"My boy, you should come work for me in Québec," Monsieur Fornac offered. "I can tell you are a trustworthy lad, and my instincts also tell me you have no fear of hard work."

"Thank you, sir," I replied. "But I journey to my father." Monsieur Fornac knew this, as the conversation was not our first on the matter.

"Ah, yes, of course," Monsieur Fornac said. He stared off to the sea. "I have no family of my own, you know. It would be welcome to have an honest sort in my confidence." His voice was gruff.

We both strolled along the deck. I listened with rapt attention as Monsieur Fornac described the settlement of Québec and what I could expect there. Visions of a vibrant and exciting life at my father's side filled my head. He had an important and powerful post there.

I noticed the walking had become more difficult and I found myself struggling to maintain an even footing. Monsieur Fornac stumbled and grasped his satchel tighter. I reached out to steady him as he slid to the railing.

Monsieur Fornac peered nervously at the water. "We're in for some weather, it seems." He laughed. But there was an edge to it.

Not a brave laugh. More like the kind of laugh one uses to make oneself brave.

It was now well after midnight. We lost the moon and the sea began to froth. "I can feel it," I said, lifting my face. "The wind, it is different."

"Yes, it comes from the north. The sea has mischief on her mind," Monsieur Fornac agreed. "I believe she means to have fun with us tonight. We should return below."

"Not yet," I said. Bad weather or not, the air was still sweet, a welcome change from the stale stench of slightly rotten food and sweat that waited below.

"Take great care," Monsieur Fornac warned. "I have travelled this voyage many times. This is not a night for stargazing." His hand swept an arc at the now starless sky. "Indeed, it is a night for nothing but hope to get through it."

Monsieur Fornac paused as he was about to leave the deck, casting a sorrowful look in my direction, as if convinced it was the last time he would ever lay eyes on me. One last shake of his head and he was gone.

The ship pitched and rolled. Icy ocean water slapped my face. I braced against the rolling deck, clinging to the ropes. Fear had not yet found me. Quite the opposite. I was exhilarated. I was a fool.

A sound like thunder erupted and a great shudder rippled through the ship as it came to a sudden stop. Cargo toppled from the deck over the side. But then, just as quickly, we were free of whatever had taken hold of us and were tossed about the waves once more.

Shouts and cries were snatched by the wind. All but one.

"The ship is taking on water!"

Monsieur Fornac reappeared at my side, his bulging satchel tight in his grasp.

"My boy, she's doomed. We must abandon ship, before she is dashed on the rocks," he cried.

"Jump into the sea? We will surely drown!"

"No, boy. See there? A boat has been ripped from the ship's moorings. But it will be lost to us if we do not act now."

Sure enough, a small boat bobbed in the waves next to the ship.

"What of the others?" I cried. Strangely, we were still alone on this section of the deck, although shouts came from all around us. "And my things..."

"There are other boats," Monsieur Fornac said. "And what worry of things, when our lives are at stake! Come now, before it is too late." He proceeded to climb over the side, tipping dangerously. He grasped my arm, and I was pulled with him.

Over the side.

We tumbled into the churning water. Nothing prepared me for the frigid iciness. Pain pierced my skin as if I was being attacked with swords. Waves crashed over my head and I was under water.

The small boat crashed into me, and I latched onto the side before it was again ripped away. I dragged myself on board, shivering and gasping for breath. It was empty.

Where was Monsieur Fornac?

Through the rain, I could see the outline of the flailing ship. Another thunderous roar bellowed through the storm as it was tossed once more upon the rocks. The mast listed wildly as the ship appeared to stagger backward, like a drunkard, its sails dipping dangerously into the waves.

Monsieur Fornac was right, the ship was doomed.

"Claude, my boy," a raspy voice called. I scanned the rough water. A pale face. An outstretched hand.

I grasped Monsieur Fornac's hand and pulled. I pitched forward, almost falling into the water. He was too heavy. "Use your other hand!" I cried. "I cannot pull you in."

"My satchel," he replied. "I cannot lift it from my side."

"Let it go!"

"I cannot. It holds my fortune. I will be destitute."

"You will be dead!" His hand slipped slightly from mine. "I cannot hold you. You must give me your other hand!"

"I've enjoyed our talks. You are a fine young man and your father is lucky to have you as a son." Monsieur Fornac squeezed my hand, then pulled his from my grasp.

"No," I cried. "What are you doing?" I lurched forward, almost capsizing.

His gaze held mine as his other arm sank beneath the water. Groaning with effort, his head thrown back, he heaved the satchel with both hands up from its watery hold. I fell back, out of the way. It crashed to the deck, splitting open, its secret contents finally exposed.

Jewels of all colours poured out at my feet, a carpet of riches.

"A king's ransom," I breathed. I looked up with a smile for Monsieur Fornac. But all that greeted me was an empty ocean.

"Monsieur Fornac?" I called

It was the sea that answered, tossing a momentous wave upon me. And my world turned upside down.

Chapter 18

"SO, MONSIEUR FORNAC...HE DIED?" Mai whispered.

Fred blinked at the sound of her voice, the spell broken. "Yeah."

"The jewels," Grace said. "Is that what you think is in that box?"

Fred nodded. "Claude talks of how the big wave washed most of the jewels overboard, but lots remained wedged in the boat. That's a whole other story. He—"

"Lost?" Grace cried. "Really?" She leapt to the top of the wall, pointing out to the sea. "Then they're still out there?"

Fred shrugged. "I guess so."

"Why are you wasting your time on a few that might be in a tiny box if there's a whole pile of jewels out there just waiting to be found? We could get a boat and diving gear and—"

Fred shook his head. "It's not that simple."

"Why not? How hard can it be? We're fossil hunters, after all."

"I read up on *Le Chameau* and the treasure. There were tons of people looking for it. It had been carrying the money for a whole year of France's expenses for their settlement in Quebec, so it was big! Way bigger than a sack full of jewels. But they searched and searched and couldn't find it."

"So those jewels weren't the real treasure?" Mai said.

"Nope. No one even knew about Fornac's jewels. The treasure from *Le Chameau* was lost for over two hundred years until it was finally discovered in the 1960s. And even then, it took them months of tracing the debris on the ocean floor to find it." Fred didn't add that he'd already been thinking about what may be at the bottom of the sea...and every possible way to get it.

"But—"

Fred held up his hand. One thing he had heard over and over from his father was how hard treasure hunting was. "Grace, the water is freezing cold, and really deep with wicked currents. Wrecks get scattered for miles, and—"

"Okay, okay," Grace griped. "I get it." She plunked down on the wall, legs dangling.

KAABOOOMM!!!

Fred ducked.

"It's just the cannon," Mai said.

Geez, why am I so jumpy? The cannon goes off a gazillion times a day. I should be used to it. "Must be all the psychos around here," Fred said. "Between that nutty soldier Gerard and wacko pirate guy, it's crazytown. And they're all after me."

"Paranoid much?" Grace said.

He scowled back at her.

"All right you two, cool it," Mai said. She stood, brushing grass from her dress. "So. Fill us in on the rest. How did the jewels get from the boat to underground at the fortress?"

"As entertaining as the history lesson is, can we skip Claude's life story for now?" asked Grace.

Fred's fingers clutched the parchment pages. Grace was right, they didn't have time for it. "I guess it doesn't matter much, does it? And none of it means anything if I don't get the box back." His guts clenched at the thought.

A strong gust of wind whipped around them, almost snatching his treasured papers from his hand.

"The weather's weird today, isn't it?" Mai said. "Hope it's not *Le Chameau* weather."

The waves were even choppier now, the peaks like snow-frosted mountains. Dark clouds were again gathering on the horizon. Fred shrugged, trying to brush off a growing feeling of dread.

"Well, we can't do anything without the box," he said. "We've got to find Lester's campsite."

Neither Grace nor Mai looked thrilled at the prospect.

"You don't have to come with me," he said.

"Yeah, like that's going to happen," Grace said with a grimace. "We stick together and that's that."

Mai nodded.

"But we should wait for Jeeter," Grace added. "He likely won't be gone much longer."

Fred shook his head. "Wasted enough time already.

He'll find us." *The longer he stays away the better,* he added silently. Fred carefully refolded the parchments, returned them to the waterproof zip-lock, and tucked them back into his waistband. He patted them protectively as he gazed up toward the King's Bastion. The hill was dotted with campsites. "Let's go," he said.

As they crossed the quay, dirt and rocks were being tossed around by the now steady wind. A baseball hat rolled by, chased by a balding tourist. Grace and Mai held down their skirts.

The restaurant was packed, with a line of people outside waiting for seats. His mother was taking orders as they walked by. She glanced up, saw them and waved. Fred waved back. She looked tired. *This is the last day you'll have to work!* he promised silently.

They continued walking. The street ended.

"I'm not crawling back into those weeds!" Grace said, pointing to the swaying, white-topped field of plants.

"Me neither," Mai said. She struggled to smooth her long hair. "Give me a sec, I've got to braid this before I lose an eye! I wish I had my backpack. I need an elastic."

"Do mine, too?" Grace said, tugging on her long ponytail.

Their voices faded as Fred surveyed the hillside. There were dozens and dozens of campsites. They all looked the same. The people were thick as ants on an anthill. How would they ever find Lester? If he was even still here. No! He was here. He had to be.

A wave of helplessness washed over him. His head felt like it was stuck in a helmet two sizes too small, his forehead pulsing. He wanted to scream and hit something. Instead, he closed his eyes and held a deep breath, letting it out slowly. *Think!*

Okay, they didn't have to check *every* site. There probably wouldn't be any kids or really old people with Lester. That had to eliminate more than half the sites right off the bat. He'd never seen so many white heads in one place before.

And likely no women either. That was kind of a big assumption to make, but they had to start somewhere. Fred figured since Lester wasn't a real re-enactor, his site would be bare, with no display stuff around it.

He opened his eyes and re-surveyed the same scene with those filters. Almost every site was elaborately set up, with a firepit and some kind of display of old-fashioned things—clothes hanging and barrels and stuff. And many also had old people doing some kind of activity, cooking or whatever.

A few sites were almost empty, with just a tent and no one around them. They'd start with those.

Another strong gust of wind whistled past. Fred glanced up, shocked to see that the boiling clouds had filled the sky and were now directly overhead. A fat raindrop landed on his cheek.

"C'mon," he said, waving them forward, his eyes fixed on the first target. Somewhere out there his box was waiting for him.

Chapter 19

THEY TRUDGED UP THE HILL, the King's Bastion looming closer, and stopped at the first target campsite. Its tent resembled their own—old and grungy. The used-to-be-white canvas was tattered and bits of mould were spreading from the corners. The poles were caked with rust.

They stood together, surveying the tent.

"Well, someone's got to check inside, right?" Grace said.

No one moved.

She sighed and stomped over, pulling aside the flap.

"What do you want?" a voice bellowed.

"Oops, sorry, wrong tent," she said, quickly backing away.

An old man emerged, pulling suspenders over his shoulders. His undershirt was as un-white as the tent, and he held a rifle in his hand. The blue wool pants indicated he was dressed up as a soldier.

"Can't a man get a nap around here?" he groused, scowling at them.

"Uh, sorry," Fred said.

They walked quickly away, the man's complaints following them. Others from nearby sites seemed to have overheard the altercation, their suspicious gazes following them.

Great, just what we need—attention, Fred thought.

"Maybe this isn't such a good idea," Mai said. She twisted her hair in her fingers, pulling it from the loose braid. "We should go back. We could get in real trouble."

"We'll be fine," Fred said. "We just have to be a bit less conspicuous."

"Well, don't blame me," Grace said. "You're the one who said we had no time."

"We won't have *any* time if we get kicked out of here," Fred said. "Let's go over to the other side of the hill, away from anyone who might have seen us."

There were fewer sites there, which meant less attention from prying eyes. A perfect place if you didn't want people to notice you. Exactly where box-stealing-criminal Lester would camp out.

"Oh, I hope the rain holds off," Mai said, as another splatter fell. She wiped at a drop running down her face. "We'll get soaked."

They approached another of the out-of-place sites that had no props around the tent. It looked abandoned. Fred walked slowly to the entrance and paused. "Um, hello?'

Silence.

"Hello," he repeated. "Is anyone in there?"

Nothing.

Cautiously he moved the flap slightly to peer inside. It was empty. Not just of people, but of anything. Totally bare. Could it have been Lester's and he'd already left? Nausea churned in his gut.

He hesitated. Should he enter?

"Moved your campsite, did ya?"

Fred jerked backward from the tent and swung around. Great. Crazy Gerard.

"Uh, no," Fred said.

"So what are you doing?" He peered past Fred toward the tent.

"Looking for a friend."

"A friend, huh?" Gerard shot Fred a skeptical look. "What friend would that be?"

Anger coiled around Fred's insides. He was getting a little tired of being pushed around. This guy was too nosy. Didn't he have work to do? "Just a friend!"

"Hmm," Gerard said.

Fred stared at him. What could this guy do to them, anyway? They hadn't done anything wrong. The more he thought about it, the madder he got. Besides, it didn't make any difference anyway. If this had been Lester's campsite, he was long gone. And Lester would have the box with him. So there was no point sticking around.

"He's probably out on one of the battles, or maybe in town," Fred said curtly. "We'll come back later." He gestured to Mai and Grace to follow him and started walking in the direction of the King's Bastion.

"Hey, I'm not done with you!" Gerard barked.

Fred didn't look back.

They had entered the gates to the bastion before Grace whistled under her breath. "Are you some kind of tough guy now?" she said. "Or some pod-hatched alien imposter? Who are you and what have you done to Freddo?"

"Ha ha," Fred laughed, "very funny." But he felt exhilarated, too. Adrenaline raced through his veins. One tiny bit of control over his out-of-control life.

In the interior courtyard of the King's Bastion, it was as if they'd stepped through a time-travel portal. Outside this main structure, you were always aware of the town's incomplete edges; its reconstructed centre seemed cocooned, as if inside a snow globe.

Here, in the enclosed quarters of the bastion, everything was more alive. Even the air felt different. Thicker. It vibrated with tension and danger. The grass-covered tops of the stone walls were guarded by patrolling men. Another group was huddled by the cannon, smoke billowing and sparks flaring. Soldiers in blue carried out musket-firing demonstrations. Acrid smoke filled the air. Shots boomed and echoed off the stone walls.

Other soldiers in red and blue carried out mock battles in the grassy courtyard, paired off in duelling blurs of colour, smaller versions of the bigger battles being staged in some of the outer fields. Insults boomed and swords clanged, all within a few feet of where Fred, Mai, and Grace stood.

KAABOOOM!

The cannon blast shook the glass windows.

Another group of re-enactors marched in through the archway, a drummer flanked by soldiers. A flute player was in the rear, the fluttering notes from his tune adding an eerie tone to the harsh rhythm of the fighting.

The spell was only broken when you turned right. Tourists lined the bastion wall in their out-of-place, bright, logoed T-shirts and garish, patterned shorts. Cameras obscured their faces as they captured the spectacle.

"Shouldn't we be looking in more tents for your friendly neighbourhood pirate?" Grace asked.

"We'll wait a couple of minutes to make sure Gerard's gone. Man, that guy's a pain in the butt. What's he got against me, anyway?"

"I chalk it up to great instincts." Grace grinned at him.

Fred scowled, which only made her grin widen. Mai was silent, staring off at nothing, chewing her thumbnail. What was up with her today?

"There you guys are."

Fred bristled at the voice.

"Where were you?" Grace asked Jeeter.

"Sorry, I didn't mean to be gone so long," he said. "But there was a cool weapons demonstration at the armory and a mock battle in the field down there. What have you been up to?"

"Fred's box was stolen from his tent! We've been looking for it," Grace said.

"Your little box was stolen? Did you find it?"

Fred hadn't minded a bit that Jeeter had been gone. And now that he was back, Fred wished he'd disappear again. "No!"

"Chill, Freddo," Jeeter said, holding up his palms. "You need to relax." He slapped Fred on the shoulder.

Fred shrugged him off. The sting of the slap lingered. What was with this guy, always punching him in the arm or hitting his shoulder? Fred's adrenaline rush at standing up to Gerard evaporated as he time-warped back to being a kindergarten pipsqueak. He opened his mouth, about to snap the insult that was on the tip of his tongue, when a familiar sight caught the corner of his eye. There. Amongst the tourists. His father was deep in conversation with Lester.

Fred's jaw clenched. The box thief. His instinct was to run to him and demand he give it back. His feet moved, as if to carry out his wish, but then he paused.

His father was shaking his head and gesturing angrily with his hands. Lester was equally angry, jabbing a pointed finger at Fred's dad. If only Fred were close enough to hear what they were saying. Urgency gripped him as the two quarrelling men turned and disappeared through the stone archway.

Mai and Grace were talking to Jeeter, all three turned away from Fred toward the battlefield. Seizing his chance, Fred stepped away, squeezing through a group of nattering senior citizens. Silently, he followed his father and the box thief into the shadowy interior of the bastion.

Chapter 20

THE BUILDING WAS VACANT, EVERYONE apparently drawn to the mock battles outside. He paused, wondering which way Lester and his dad had gone.

Loud voices drew him toward the chapel.

He peered around the corner into the brightly lit room. The walls were plastered white, with skylights and windows letting in enough daylight to illuminate every corner, even under the gloomy clouds. There were no places to hide. But there was no sign of his father or the box thief. Suddenly, though, he could hear them.

"Pete, you're out of time," Lester said.

"Look, I explained it to you," his dad replied. "The delays couldn't be helped. We're still a go for tonight. And it's looking good."

Fred surveyed the room. Where were the voices coming from? He turned around and went back into the hallway.

There was no sign of the pair, nor could he hear them. He returned to the chapel, and the voices were clear as a bell. Where were they?

"Why don't you give me the details on what you have so far?" Lester said. "I need this. If you don't deliver..."

The threat hung in the air.

"Patience. We're a go for the boat tonight. It'll take us right to it."

"We'll never get a chance like this again!" Lester said, his voice louder.

"Take it easy, Lester," Fred's dad said. "You'll get what's coming to you."

"I'd better."

The door to the confessional cracked open, and the curtain on the other side also moved.

Overcome with an instinct to hide, Fred retreated from the room and ducked into a nearby stairwell. Pressed against the wall, he held his breath. Footsteps echoed off the stone and faded away. His heartbeat throbbed in his ears. Fred waited another full minute, and then poked his head into the tunnel. The coast was clear.

Sighing with relief at escaping detection, he couldn't resist one more look to see where they were headed. He exited the bastion and stood on the wooden bridge over the weed-filled former moat. The men had separated, Lester the box thief turning toward the campsites on the hill, and his dad veering toward the museum and the ruins down the hill to the right of town.

His eyes instinctively followed Lester as he trudged through the various sites and entered the same empty tent Fred had searched earlier. Lester must have kept the box with him.

It seemed from the conversation with his dad that whatever Lester was up to, he couldn't have opened the box. That made sense, didn't it? He'd have been talking about it if he had, wouldn't he? Not about some boat. So, Fred still had time. While his brain was busily formulating a plan, he walked slowly, returning to the crowds and noise of the bastion courtyard.

"So, what's the plan?" Grace asked. They were strolling back down the hill toward town.

Fred hadn't gotten far with the actual planning part of the plan, so he really had nothing to offer. "I'm thinking."

"Uh-huh," Grace said. "Translation: not a sweet clue."

Fred scowled. Grace was annoying sometimes. Make that a lot of the time. "Well, why don't you come up with something?"

"I would, Freddo, no problem, but you haven't told us what the heck is going on around here!"

"What do you mean?"

"We're not blind," Grace said. "We saw your dad with that Lester creep."

"And we saw you follow them," Mai added softly, "without us."

He felt a flush stain his face. "Yeah, about that—"

"If he's working with your dad, then why don't you ask your dad about your box?" Jeeter suggested. "He'd be the logical choice, right?"

Fred frowned at Jeeter.

"Hey, I'm just saying," Jeeter said.

Fred didn't answer, staring instead at the harbour. They were back on the quay. The tall ships were visiting as part of the encampment, half a dozen of them anchored in the harbour. Would his dad have been talking about one of those boats? There were no others in the harbour, so it would have to be one of them. He just had to find out which one.

"Freddy," a soft voice said.

He whipped around. "Mom?"

She was as white and pasty as uncooked dough. Tendrils of her hair had escaped her bonnet and clung limply to her damp forehead. She grasped his sleeve. Her hand was shaking.

"I think I overdid it," she said shakily. "I need to lie down for a minute."

He thought of the heaping pile he'd left in his tent. "C'mon, I'll take you. Mai, I'm going to put her in yours, okay?"

Mai's brown eyes, full of concern, met his. "Of course." She gently took his mom's other arm and they guided her the short distance to their site.

Grace pulled back the tent flap. "Um, excuse my mess," she said, grabbing clothes off the floor on her side of the tent and tossing them to the corner.

Mai helped his mom to her sleeping bag, neatly arranged on the floor. His mom sighed and closed her eyes, draping her arm across her forehead. "Don't let me sleep more than fifteen minutes," she said, her voice already thick and sluggish. Within seconds, her breathing was slow and deep.

Grace went back outside, leaving Fred and Mai inside with his sleeping mother. Fred flopped down onto Grace's crumpled sleeping bag. He felt winded, like he'd just run a race.

Mai's hair brushed against his face as she sat down beside him. She wrapped her arms around her bent legs and rested her chin on her knees. They watched his mom as she slept.

"Why didn't you tell me about your mom?"

Fred could hear the hurt in Mai's voice. "I'm sorry."

"I'm your best friend. I could have helped."

Fred sighed. "I know."

"So why didn't you?"

He searched for the words. His thoughts from the past two months were all crammed together in his head, like a pile of dirty laundry stuffed in a hamper. He struggled to pull them apart. Into something that made sense.

"It was so weird," he said. That was lame. Not really what he meant, either. "I mean, it came out of nowhere. It was suppertime. Mom was sitting in the lawnchair wrapped in a blanket. I was barbecuing hamburgers and she says, 'The cancer is back,' as if she was asking me to pass the ketchup." He heard his voice, raspy and uneven.

Mai reached out and squeezed his hand.

"She said she had felt something was wrong for a while, that it might be back, but she'd been afraid to get tested. She was catching every cold, everything that was going around all winter. Her immune system was toast. I was out spelunking in sinkholes without a care in the world and Mom had cancer."

"That's not your fault. You didn't know."

Blood rushed to his head. Fred sucked in a deep breath and blew it out slowly. "Then I kept thinking, you know, how we saved Grace's dad and everything. I felt like…I felt like all the 'save the parents' luck had been used up, you know? I mean, what were the odds both of them would be okay? Grace's dad *and* my mom? I couldn't face you guys. I couldn't face Grace's happy ending day after day. Not while I was looking after Mom."

"It's okay."

Tears leaked from his eyes and his throat burned. "Mom didn't have any benefits from the bakery. No sick days. No insurance. And Dad was self-employed. She was so sick from the pneumonia, she could hardly get out of bed. It was like that for weeks. I was doing everything—cooking, laundry, all of it. Then the dive shop closed a couple of weeks ago out of the blue. Dad's contract he'd been working on was cancelled."

Mai sniffed and brushed her free hand across her face, squeezing his hand tighter. Fred turned to look at her and saw her cheeks were wet, too.

Thunder crashed overhead. Rain erupted and pelted the tent, a ceaseless drum roll. His mother didn't stir.

"You know, at first Mom said she wasn't going to get any treatment. That she couldn't go through it again. Said she wasn't strong enough. She was talking about just enjoying our time together, however long that was." His breath caught on the sob that burst from him. "I hadn't asked her about it. But I knew it must have been bad...the last time."

"Oh, Fred," Mai whispered.

"She kept these journals. In a box in her closet. One afternoon when she was sleeping on the couch, I searched through them and found it. The one from the last time she had cancer. It was all in there. How she'd thrown up all the time and been so sick she could barely lift her head. The pain. How much she cried. And she wrote lots of times that it wasn't worth living. That if she survived, she'd never do it again."

"Your poor mom."

"It was awful! How could I ask her to go through that again? But she felt bad about her decision, I know she did. Couldn't look at me without tears in her eyes. She got really depressed. She hardly ate and she slept all the time. I think that's partly why she had pneumonia for so long. But then a couple of weeks ago, something changed. She seemed to come around."

He stared out at the rain. "It's weird, like when things were the worst, when Dad's business went under, she came out of this fog she was in. And last week she finally said yes. They're going to start treatments right away. I think...I think she wants to fight, because...because maybe she thinks Dad can't look after me."

Mai gasped, her hand covering her mouth. "You really think that?"

"I don't know. Maybe it isn't that. It could be it took her awhile to get ready for it in her mind, you know? Like getting ready for battle or something. I guess it doesn't matter why, just that she's going to do it. Fight. But that's why I've got to get my box back, Mai," he said. Conviction surged through him like a fever. "Mom will be able to go to one of those places like the Mayo Clinic or something. Get the best, you know? And she won't have to worry about working, or money. It'll fix everything."

Chapter 21

GRACE POKED HER FACE INSIDE the tent. Her hair was plastered to her head and water was streaming down her face. "Uh, a little wet out here."

"Come in," Mai said. Her voice was shaking and she was gripping Fred's hand tighter.

Grace looked from Mai to Fred, to their still-clasped hands, and back to Mai. "No, that's okay. I'm going over to Jeeter's. He's got food. Want anything?"

Fred shook his head and Grace was gone again. He stood up and looked outside. People were running toward buildings, holding backpacks and purses over their heads. The few who had umbrellas were walking awkwardly, trying to hold onto them in the wind gusts. A flash of lightning zigzagged across the sky, followed by another crash of thunder. That got the umbrella-holders hustling faster for cover, too.

Mai murmured, "One one thousand, two one—"

Another flash of forked lightning hit somewhere up to their left. "Wow, it's pretty wild out there!" Fred said.

"Are we safe?"

"We should be."

"But aren't these poles made of metal?" Mai pointed at the ceiling.

Fred followed her gaze. A shiver of alarm ran up his spine. A TV show he'd seen recently popped into his head. Lightning had struck tents in a campground in Ontario. One man had died and a bunch had been injured. He imagined what it must feel like to have that much energy frying your insides, and shuddered.

"Maybe you're right." He went over and shook his mom's arm gently. She didn't stir. "Mom, wake up."

She was sleeping like the dead. And no way was he leaving her alone. That storm had been far away, he reasoned. It had likely been way worse than this one. They even got tornadoes up there in Ontario. He flinched at another crack of thunder. And what were the odds of the same thing happening again? They'd be fine, right?

He and Mai huddled inside the tent, watching the sheets of rain bounce off the gravel. Gusts of wind buffeted the tent and the rusty poles shook. Leaks sprung in the canvas. Another crack of thunder echoed like a cannon shot. His mother didn't wake up.

"Your mom must be really tired," Mai said.

"She's still so wiped from having pneumonia," Fred said. "And with her treatments starting, she needs to build up her strength. That's what burns me. She should be home, not here."

"It'll work out."

"It will when I get my box back. Then we'll have enough money and Mom can stay home. It won't matter about not having sick days or insurance then."

Mai bit her lip. "But…if you find it. And you open it. And it really is some kind of treasure. You can't keep it. You'll get in trouble—for stealing."

"*Stealing?* What are you talking about?" Fred said. His voice got louder. Did saying it louder make it true? "I read you the journal. Those jewels belong to my family."

His mother moaned and rolled onto her side. Fred knelt beside her and touched her arm. "Mom?"

Her breathing immediately returned to a deep rhythm. She was still asleep. A new leak in the tent began dripping water close to her face. He grabbed a pot from the cooking supplies and put it underneath.

Tap. Tap. Tap.

He sat back on his haunches, watching her sleep. The dark, purplish bruises under her eyes looked like smudged chalk. He wished they were chalk and then he could erase them away. But it wasn't as easy as that. Nothing was.

"Fred," Mai said, "don't get mad. I'm only worried about you. I mean, it's the government. They own this place, and everything in it…and under it. I don't think they'd be convinced by some old journal. And besides, what you read to us proves they *weren't* his jewels."

"Fornac gave them to Claude!"

"Well..." Mai hedged.

"Anyway, who's going to know?" Fred asked. "Are you going to tell?" He tilted his head to look at her.

Mai held his gaze. "No," she said softly. "Of course not. But I've got to—"

"Hey," Grace said, reappearing at the tent opening. "Sorry to interrupt. I need to change. I'm soaked."

Fred held a finger to his lips and pointed at his mother.

"Oops, sorry," she said as she stooped low and slipped inside.

"You aren't interrupting," Mai said.

Not interrupting? He'd been spilling his guts. Private stuff. How was that not interrupting? Fred clenched his teeth.

Mai stuck her head outside. "I see blue sky."

Fred opened the flap further. Sure enough, the rain was easing off and there were splotches of blue sky farther out over the harbour. "Just a thundershower," he said, relieved. But he noticed there were more dark clouds off in the distance.

With the wind dying down, the tall ships were almost still on the already calmer water. Which one of them had his dad been talking about? The one they were going on tonight?

His dad's conversation from last night with Lester replayed in his head. It was weird. But his dad had said something about "invictum." Could that be the name of a ship or something? It sounded familiar, like he'd heard the name somewhere else. No, that wasn't right. Not heard. Maybe read it?

He shook his head, hoping it would rattle the scattered pieces into place. The brochures about the fortress. Where were they? He slipped out of Mai and Grace's tent and entered his own. Everything was still piled high. A Mount Everest of junk. He dug through and found his duffle bag. He pulled the clothes out, and there, crumpled in the bottom, were a handful of coloured pamphlets.

He flipped open the one on the grand encampment. Inside was a list of activities. He scanned it. "Tour a tall ship." That was it! He read the description:

Take a sail and experience the high seas of the 1700s. The Invictum *is a replica of a ship that sailed in 1758. Sunset cruise Saturday at 6 p.m.*

That was tonight. Murmured voices were coming from the other tent. His mom must be awake, finally. He was folding the brochure when he noticed another activity listed. A late-night lantern tour of the fortress. There were also workshops on baking bread and blacksmithing. The forge! The fires were made to melt metal. Why hadn't he thought of that before? That's how he could get into the box. His heartbeat quickened.

Inside the tent, his mother was sitting up, talking with Mai. She still looked pasty, but her eyes were bright. She smiled up at him.

"You're feeling better?" he asked.

She nodded slowly. "Definitely. One hundred percent better!"

"Do you want me to find Dad so he can take you home?"

"Take me home?"

"Mom, you're not going back to work. You have to go home!"

His mom smoothed out her hair and adjusted her bonnet. "I can't do that." She held her hand out and automatically Fred reached over and grabbed it, hauling her to her feet. She swayed slightly and gripped his arm.

"Mom."

"It'll be fine. I was just doing too much."

"You should—"

She patted his hand. "Don't worry about me."

Fred grunted. She wasn't fine. Not by a long shot. But what could he do? Until he had the jewels in his hands, there was no way for him to help.

"Although, now that you mention it, maybe you could do something for me," his mom said.

Well, he could at least walk her back over to work. "No problem," he said, ready to escort her from the tent.

She smiled. "You can help me in the restaurant since you're in costume. Carry the trays, clean a few tables. That's what was too much for me, carrying those heavy trays. It'll be fun."

Fred gulped. "Work in the restaurant?"

"This is wonderful," she beamed. "Things happen for a reason."

Fred opened his mouth to protest. But how could he refuse? She needed him. He was trapped.

Chapter 22

"CAN YOU CLEAR TABLE FIVE?" his mother said as she passed by him. He was already clearing from a family of eight whose kids must have been farm animals in disguise. *Did they eat anything?* he wondered, disgusted. He pulled a spoon covered in sticky apple tart goop from the tablecloth and tossed it onto the tray, then bent to scrape up a piece of meat pie that had been smeared into the wooden floor. There seemed to be more food on the table and floor than had been delivered. Kids were pigs.

"I'll get it," Mai said. She delivered a tray of food to a waiting table and continued to the recently vacated one.

There was a lineup at the door and past the window. People were glaring at him. "Hurry up!" their eyes said.

The afternoon had been a sweaty blur. His arms and back ached. And his feet were throbbing. The stupid wooden shoes were killing him! And the wool pants were torture, making him itch in places he couldn't scratch in public. Sweat dripped from his forehead and down his back. It streamed from under his arms, between his legs, and leaked between his toes. He was one big sponge being squeezed of every last drop of water.

"We're out of linens," his mom said. There was no gratitude in her eyes for him. She, too, was trapped in the sweaty horror that was the restaurant. They were all in survival mode. "Can you take over the dirty ones and get a fresh batch from Jeanette?"

Grateful for the chance to get outside for even a minute, Fred nodded. He cleared the rest of the table and reset it, then dropped off the tray in the kitchen. The dishwasher and cook barely glanced up, their hair matted to their foreheads under their caps, faces bright red and glistening. No one was having fun today.

"Linen?" he asked.

The guy closest to him swung his arm behind him, a vague gesture to the corner. Fred grabbed the stuffed bag, heaved it over his shoulder, and headed out the back door, stopping for a second in front of the one and only fan.

"Hey, you're blocking the air!" came an instant protest.

"Sorry," he muttered.

Outside wasn't much better. Maybe worse. It was as if the entire fortress had been shoved under a heat lamp. Not a breath of wind stirred. Waves of heat radiated up from the ground.

The harbour was still, the ships perfectly reflected in the water. Part of Fred's brain registered it. Thought it would make a great photograph. Then it was taken over by a dream of jumping into the cool water, and sticking his head under, and swimming along the bottom like Aquaman. He could swim all the way to the North Pole. Sit on an iceberg.

Another drop of sweat dripped into his eye, burning. The fantasy ruined, he was back in the oven. He trudged over to the neighbouring building and yanked open the back door. "Hey, Jeanette," he said, dumping the bag onto the floor. "Clean ones?"

"There," she said, gesturing to a neatly folded stack of white tablecloths and napkins. "It's a scorcher, isn't it!" She wiped her sleeve across her forehead. "Someone said it's over forty with the humidity."

"Wicked," he agreed.

He'd already been to the laundry earlier. Tall and pretty Jeanette was really nice to him.

"Got something for you," she said, beckoning him over. She disappeared through a side door and reappeared with her hands behind her back. "Don't tell anyone."

She held up two cans of pop. Fred blinked, reaching out to take one. The can was icy cold. He held it to his forehead. "Ahhh," he sighed, rolling it down the side of his face. He popped the tab and took a long, deep drink. The cola bubbles fizzed inside his mouth.

"How's that?" Jeanette said, her own head tilted back to take a drink.

He chugged the remainder of the can, his eyes watering. "Awesome!" he gasped.

BBRRAAAWWP!

Jeanette laughed at his belch. "Sure hits the spot, doesn't it?"

He nodded.

She brushed her hair from her face and drained her can, too. "Here, give me the evidence." She took the cans and put them back in the cooler, covered it, and shut the door. "What they don't know won't hurt them." She winked at him.

He laughed and picked up the stack of linen. "Later," he called over his shoulder.

Back at the restaurant, he dumped the clean stack in the kitchen, grabbed a tray, and headed into the dining room. It was even busier than when he'd left. Mai was clearing a table near the front door, saw him looking her way, and smiled. She was the only one in here who didn't look like she'd been dunked in a steam bath.

Grace and Jeeter were off somewhere. A flash of resentment washed over him. Wherever they were, it had to be better than here. It definitely had to be cooler. He couldn't blame them, he supposed. If it hadn't been his mother who had asked, would he be in this inferno? Not a chance.

And where was his dad? He hadn't seen him since the chapel. What time was it, anyway? Not wearing a watch was driving him crazy. No wristwatches back in the 1700s, so it couldn't be part of the costume. It was easy to lose track of time. Which usually meant it passed by fast.

But today, he was so miserable and uncomfortable that the time had dragged. Even though he'd been "busier than a one-armed paper hanger," as his grandfather used to say.

He'd been forced to ask diners for the time now and then to keep track. Even now, a tourist at the front of the line was pointedly looking at his watch and at the empty table Mai was clearing.

Fred strode over to him and smiled. "We'll get you a seat in just a minute, sir."

The man's face softened slightly. "Thank you."

"Could you tell me the time?"

"Half past five."

Oh no! The restaurant was full. Empty tables were piled high with dirty dishes. The tour was at six o'clock! He'd told Grace about the tour before coming to the restaurant, so she and Jeeter were likely already waiting there. He gazed out the window at the harbour. The sun was lower now, the shadows a bit longer. Ships waited, as if holding their breath, on the still water. One of them was the *Invictum*. He had to get on that boat.

But it may as well have been a million miles away.

Chapter 23

TIME WAS PASSING. THE MAN who'd told him the time was now seated and had ordered. The restaurant was open until nine o'clock, Fred knew that, and the line at the door was still long. His mother was working, but taking longer and longer breaks, sitting on the corner stool in the kitchen. So he couldn't escape that way. His agitation grew by the second. How was he going to get out of here?

Mai was all smiles, looking the same as she had all day. Not a bead of sweat in sight. She finished loading her tray with another stack of dirty dishes. His mother had re-emerged and was taking an order from a large table.

This was his chance! He grabbed the tray from Mai. "I'll take it."

She shot him a small smile. "Thanks."

He returned the smile and headed back to the kitchen.

The poor dishwasher and cook looked like they'd been partly melted, as if the heat had rendered them, shrinking them like frying bacon.

They didn't look up. The back door was open. Could it be that easy? He dropped the tray of dishes by the sink, mumbled something about garbage and slipped outside. He glanced back, guilt washing over him at leaving Mai and his mother behind.

But what could he do? He couldn't get Mai to come with him without his mother noticing. And then he'd run the risk of not getting out at all. Besides, his mom would need Mai's help, especially with him gone.

Fred dashed around the building and raced to his tent. Grace and Jeeter were sitting by the empty firepit in front of the two tents, wearing regular clothes—shorts and tees. Lucky them.

"It's about time," Grace said.

"We gotta go," he said, zooming past them and into his tent. He kicked the wooden shoes into the air and pulled off the thick socks. He wiggled his toes on the canvas. It felt deliciously cool as the sweat evaporated from his skin. Would they let him go barefoot on the tour? He scooped a pair of crumpled shorts and a T-shirt from the floor.

Nuts! A detail he'd forgotten. The tour was free for the volunteer re-enactors, but only if they were in costume. Tourists had to pay. And he had no money. He picked up the damp wool socks and gave then a sniff.

No way was he putting them back on. He shoved his bare feet into the wooden clogs. His toes were not happy.

He grabbed his backpack, but realized that wasn't part of the costume, either.

He went outside and held his pack out. "Grace, can you take this?"

"Can't! I've got my own." She patted her pack already slung over her shoulder. "You carry it."

"It's not part of the costume," Fred said. "Hey, wait a second. How come you two aren't in costume?"

Grace's face turned pink. "Um, we bought tickets so we wouldn't have to."

Fred frowned, totally ticked. But could he blame them? He didn't want to be in costume either. "Well, do you really need your pack?"

"What's in yours besides junk?" Grace said. "Not good junk, either. You don't even have your choco stash. That, I might consider worth it."

"You're a real pal," Fred said.

Jeeter held out his hand. "I'll take it."

Fred hesitated. The last person he wanted help from was Jeeter. But he didn't have much choice—he'd need the pack to hide his box once he got it back. Anyway, it was better than having to ask Jeeter or Grace to pay for a ticket on the boat tour so he could wear his own clothes.

"Thanks." Reluctantly, he passed the backpack to Jeeter.

"No prob, Freddo."

Fred bristled but returned the grin. Well, it was more like a grimace, but it was the best he could do. Jeeter irked him, even when he was doing something nice.

"Where's Mai?" Grace asked. "We were going to get her

a ticket for the boat tour, too, but I figured she was going for the authentic experience. Staying in character and all that." Grace shuddered. "Not me! I couldn't stand that dress a second longer."

"She's still at the restaurant. I snuck out the back."

"You left her there?" Grace said. "She's going to kill you!"

Fred shrugged, guilt curdling his stomach. "There was nothing I could do."

They started walking toward the Frédéric Gate on the quay. A huge, yellow wooden archway, it was a focal point on the shoreline road of the fortress. The large, fence-like red doors stood open, allowing access to the rocky beach. A longboat was moored at the wharf. A second was already out in the harbour, probably headed to the *Invictum*.

A fortress employee in blue soldier garb was facing away from him.

"Is there still room?" Fred asked.

The employee turned around.

Crazy Gerard.

It figured.

"Well, well," Gerard smirked. "Let me check." He stared at the list in his hand, his eyebrows mashed together. "Hmmm," he added, rubbing his chin.

Fred hopped from one foot to the other and pointed to the empty seats. "The boat's almost empty," he said.

"Yeah, but people paid in advance."

"Oh," Fred replied, his hope shrivelling.

"Don't cry," Gerard said. "Some pay and then don't show up. Hang around and there might be space left."

Fred glanced anxiously up and down the quay, watching for tourists headed their way. It looked good until a family of four came into view from around the corner. They were walking quickly toward the dock.

"Hurry up," the mother urged. "We're late!" They rushed past, with Gerard taking their tickets and crossing them off his list. Fred noticed there were several more names not crossed off. So Gerard hadn't been lying.

The longboat still had lots of room, even counting the latecomers.

The minutes ticked by. Fred was getting more anxious as the tourists dribbled in by ones and twos. The boat was almost full now. Grace and Jeeter had taken their seats already. They'd even tried to pay for a seat for Fred, but it was sold out.

"It's just a boat tour," Gerard said, seeming to notice Fred's distress from his twitching. "What's the big deal—something going on?"

"No big deal." Fred shrugged, trying to throw off the tension and relax.

Gerard didn't look convinced. "Uh-huh."

Fred's father wasn't on the boat at the dock. He must have been on the other one that had left before Fred got there. Lester the box thief too, he guessed. Either that or he was totally on the wrong track and they weren't even on the *Invictum*.

No. He had to be right. They were on board the *Invictum*. And he was getting on that boat, too.

Fred jerked his arm. Someone or something had poked

him. Hard. He swung around. Angry Mai glared at him. "You left me."

"Uh, sorry?" he sputtered. What could he say?

She thrust her hands out, face-up, under his nose. "Just look at my hands. They're a wreck. Stupid splintery trays."

"Sorry," he repeated.

"All afternoon I helped you in that restaurant. And you just took off."

"Mai, I couldn't miss the tour."

"We could have talked about it at least. If there hadn't been a way for both of us to leave, I would have stayed anyway."

Fred glanced back in the direction of the restaurant. More people were hurrying their way. Rats! "So, how did you?"

"How did I what?"

"Get away."

"Oh, they got more workers in for the supper shift."

"Oh," Fred said. He was only half-listening now, his attention on the approaching group. One, two, three...six! There were only six seats left on the longboat.

"Hold the boat!" a bald man with purple shorts yelled. "We have tickets." He was waving something in his hand.

Gerard took the offered tickets and checked off four names. They scurried past and were helped on board by another fortress worker.

The other two people had cash in their hands. "Can we get on?"

Gerard looked at the money and then at Fred. What was he going to do? Fred pleaded with his eyes.

Gerard made a big deal of studying the list in his hand again. "Sorry," he said finally, "it's sold out."

The disappointed couple turned and walked away.

Fred wondered what the catch was. More torture from crazy Gerard? Was he letting him think he'd get on, only to stop him at the last minute?

"Go on, we're not going to hold it any later. It's already quarter after six," Gerard said gruffly, waving them toward the boat. "And stay out of trouble. Though that might be a tall order. Seems to follow you around."

"Thanks!" Fred said. Maybe crazy Gerard wasn't such a jerk after all.

Fred grabbed Mai's hand and pulled her along as he raced over to board the boat before Gerard could change his mind. He jumped down, wobbling as the boat swayed with his weight.

"I knew you'd get on!" Grace said, smacking his shoulder. "Or I'd have given you my seat."

Yeah, right!

Fred and Mai took their seats and within seconds the longboat was pushing away from the dock. Fred could see swaying clumps of seaweed on the rocky bottom. A crab scuttled by, startled by the boat. The fortress workers dipped their oars into the smooth water. Fred let out his held breath as they headed toward the *Invictum*.

Finally, something was going right.

Chapter 24

CREW HANDS WERE CRAWLING OVER the rigging—a mind-boggling circus routine of leaping, swinging acrobats. Tourists lined the railings, some captivated by the crew's antics and others taking pictures of the fortress from their unique view.

The guy running the tour had said it could be cancelled if they didn't get some wind. No wind. No sail. *We need wind. We need wind.* As if in answer to Fred's silent plea, a slight breeze rippled the water. It felt good on the back of his hot neck. But would it be enough to move the *Invictum*?

The hull of the ship loomed high as they came alongside it. Barnacles clung to the wood along and below the waterline, some with small bits of seaweed attached to them.

One of the workers stood on the side of the longboat, grabbed a thrown rope to tie them on, and began guiding people up the rope ladder. Fred wiggled his toes, not excited about scaling the side of a ship in wooden clogs.

The man holding the ladder seemed to read Fred's mind.

"Those will be slippery on the ladder," he said, pointing at Fred's feet. "If you want, you can leave them here. You won't need them on board. The crew goes barefoot all the time."

"Great!" Fred didn't need a second invitation, kicking off the shoes. Mai did the same, but tucked her clogs neatly under the seat.

Fred scrambled up the ladder after Mai as it twisted to and fro. He grasped the rough rope and his bare toes curled around the rungs as he climbed. Relief washed over him when his feet hit the wooden deck. He'd made it. Fred held up his arms, the breeze cooling his sweaty underarms. The ripples in the water had quickly become small waves. The ship swayed. They had wind.

"So, what's the plan?" Grace asked.

"Find Lester. Get my box back. That's it."

"Simple plan, Freddo. I'm usually a fan of simple. But it's a little light on the details. Meaning, there are none. How exactly are we going to do that?" Grace said.

Fred surveyed the deck. There was no sign of his dad or Lester anywhere. Not a good start. But they could be on a tour below decks, or maybe in the captain's cabin, the large structure that took up the entire back half of the deck, with just a thin strip of decking along the railing on either side.

"Uh," Fred said. They'd have to search the ship, somehow. But were they allowed below decks? How many hands worked on this boat, anyhow? With other re-enactors on board from the fortress, it was hard to tell. Except for the acrobats in the air, that is. They scrambled about, unfurling the sails as if in time to a silent tune.

There was a steady wind now, the waves choppy and whitecapped again. Boy, that had happened fast. The sea had been so smooth only minutes before. It was unpredictable. Off in the distance the dark clouds seemed to loom larger than before.

Creee. Creee. Creee.

A bald eagle screeched as it glided over them. Its white head and tail feathers were bright and its dark wings gleamed in the sunlight. Fast as lightning, it dove beside the ship, talons outstretched. Water exploded as it snatched a fat fish and immediately started to climb. The *whoosh* of its wings was drowned out by the *oohs* and *ahhs* surrounding him as the tourists pointed and tried, vainly, to capture the scene on their cameras. The fish wiggled uselessly, its fate already sealed.

Fred scrunched his toes against the smooth, wooden deck, sucking in a gulp of salty ocean air. He watched until the bird was out of sight, feeling a lingering sympathy for the helpless fish. Did it know it was the end?

"My goodness, you young ones do get around, don't you?"

Fred started, shielding his eyes as he looked up. Flyaway grey hair poked out from underneath a floppy Tilley hat. It was the archaeologist from the museum. "Hi, err, Mrs.…" It was M- something or other.

The archaeologist frowned. "Enthusiastic, but not the greatest memory, hmmm? It's Molly, dear. Just Molly."

Fred's face flushed. It felt like he was being chastised by his mother for doing something wrong. "Hi, Molly," he murmured.

Her face immediately changed into a wide grin. "So good to see you all here. It's nice that the young people have an interest in all the activities." Blue eyes held his gaze in an unblinking stare. "It was a full year in the planning, you know."

"Oh, really?" Fred felt like a bug with its wings pinned to a collector's board. "Um, well, it's all great. You organized everything?"

"Yes, even this tour. It was my idea. Kind of a once-in-a-lifetime thing. The board thought it was too much, but I insisted. Adds to the experience, don't you think? And it's a special privilege—you can't travel in the coastal waters around here without clearance from the fortress officials. Did you know that?"

He shook his head.

"There are many wrecks beneath the waves here, all belonging to the park." She lowered her voice to a whisper and winked. "Some are rumoured to still hold undiscovered treasures." Molly stretched her arm out over the side. "I'm in charge of that, too. It's illegal to dive here without permission," she said. "And I don't give that out…ever. Not to civilians, anyway."

"I saw a sign that said the harbourmaster was in charge of diving."

"The harbourmaster and I are one and the same now. Cutbacks and all that. I run all the excavation activities of the fortress assets, both above and below the sea," she said.

Fred thought of his dad's night dives and mysterious activities. A tingling of alarm ran through him. Maybe she was already on to his dad? Fred knew whatever his dad was up to wasn't on the up and up. And she said she never gave out permits.

It now seemed even more important to find his box. Whatever his dad was up to, Fred knew it had to be some scheme. He always had good intentions, but they never worked out. But no matter what, Fred didn't want his dad getting into trouble. Plus, that would be one more thing for his mom to handle. And she already had enough on her plate.

So he'd have to kill two birds with one stone—get his box from Lester and warn his dad about Molly. Stop him from whatever crazy plan he'd cooked up. It had to be diving for treasure on some wreck where he wasn't allowed.

But to stop his dad, Fred had to find him.

The sails billowed, the anchor was pulled, and the *Invictum* began to move. In seconds, they were cutting through the waves in the harbour, heading out to sea. A thrill ran through Fred as the ship creaked and groaned. It was like an animal. He could feel its power beneath his feet.

He walked the length of the ship, peering into openings and dark alcoves. Then he rounded the back of the captain's cabin, about to head along the other side. Out of the corner of his eye he caught a blur of black. In a sea of cut-off tan pants and white shirts, black stood out. His dad always wore black.

Chapter 25

FRED SLIPPED INTO THE SHADOWED alcove of the captain's cabin after his dad. He squinted in the low light, almost missing the first stair. He stumbled and his shoulder slammed into the wall. Grunting, he righted himself, and peered down into the gloom.

A lantern at the bottom of the stairs cast flickering light onto the walls. The hall branched right and left. Stepping carefully, he descended into the bowels of the ship.

"Psst!"

He jumped, almost stumbling again.

"It's just me," Mai whispered.

"And me," Grace added.

"And me," Jeeter said.

"Great," Fred grumbled, "the gang's all here."

"You took off on us again!" Grace said.

Fred didn't reply and paused on the stairs. It was fine for *him* to follow his dad. But it was a different story for the rest of them. What if they found out his dad was doing something wrong, maybe even something illegal? Could he trust them?

His breath caught. He couldn't believe not trusting his friends would pop into his head. Where had that thought come from? Well, he reasoned, for sure he didn't trust Jeeter. Mai, of course. Grace? Mostly.

Someone poked him in the shoulder. "Are we going to stay on the stairs all day or what?" Grace asked.

Fred shrugged off the finger and descended to the next step. "You guys should go back."

"What?" Mai asked.

No way would she understand. Neither would Grace, for that matter—this was something Fred needed to do on his own. It hadn't really hit him until now. Their fathers were, well, cool. Grace's dad was awesome—a scientist who ran the fossil centre. He didn't know Mai's dad that well. They didn't go to her house much, usually hanging out at Grace's. But he could tell Mai's dad was awesome by the way she talked about him.

Fred had never felt that way about his own dad. The dad who was always chasing an imaginary pot of gold. It was... embarrassing. He guessed that's probably why he almost never had his friends over to his house, not that his dad was home that much anyway.

"I said you guys should go back," he repeated.

"Why?" Mai asked.

"Because it's a big ship, so we should split up. Cover more ground that way. We can regroup in a half hour or so and compare notes."

"Hey, man, this is your party," Jeeter said. "Whatever."

Grace looked like she was about to say something, then seemed to decide against it. She pressed her lips together, spun around, and followed Jeeter back up the stairs.

Mai didn't move. "I'm coming with you."

"Mai—"

"I don't care what you say, I'm not leaving."

Fred sighed. "Fine."

"I didn't see any *No entry* signs, so we should be okay," Mai said.

As long as they weren't breaking rules, Mai was fine.

"C'mon," Fred said.

They crept down the remaining stairs to the first deck below. Their bare feet were silent; the only sound was their breathing. And heartbeats. Fred's heart was playing the bongos.

At the bottom, he stood for a moment, listening for his dad. Muffled voices were coming from somewhere close by. He couldn't tell which direction. If he had had a coin, he could've flipped it to decide. But with only lint lining his pockets, he arbitrarily swung left.

The corridor was long and narrow, seeming to run almost the length of the ship. Behind them, the stairs continued to more lower decks. There were several rooms, some with closed doors and others with either open doors or none. They were sitting ducks here. Crew could appear at any moment and they'd be discovered.

The wood was smooth, but slightly uneven under their feet, with worn grooves from many feet over many years. It all gleamed, clearly polished and well cared for. No peeling paint or broken boards. The first door had a brass doorknob. Fred pressed his ear to it, but heard nothing. He turned the knob. Locked. Two more rooms with open doors were empty. Then another locked one, with no sounds coming from inside.

The voices he'd heard had faded. Clearly, he'd picked the wrong direction. He was turning toward Mai when the thunder of footsteps echoed on the stairs.

Mai gasped, grabbing his sleeve.

Panicked, he took her hand and pulled her with him into the last open doorway they'd passed, shutting the door silently behind them. He felt for a lock. There was none. They'd have to hope this room wasn't the destination. The interior was dimly lit from a lamp on a large desk covered with maps. The far wall was a floor-to-ceiling bookcase. Two crossed swords gleamed on the dark wooden wall above their heads.

"Fred."

"Shhh," he whispered, holding his finger to Mai's lips. He froze. Her lips were soft against the side of his finger. She didn't pull away.

They didn't move as the footsteps came closer. Fred held his breath as they paused, then carried on past them. He heard the clang of keys and the slam of a door.

"Can I talk now?" Mai asked. Her lips tickled his skin.

"Uh, sure."

She moved back and he lowered his hand.

"C'mon," he said, exiting and hurrying quietly in the opposite direction. He stopped short of the stair entrance. He peeked up to make sure no one was coming down. They scurried past the opening and continued down the hallway.

Immediately, he heard the voices again. He stopped. Mai bumped into the back of him.

"Sorry."

He began moving forward again. Slowly. He tried to pinpoint the source of the voices. It was a bit further down the hall.

"Fred?"

"What?"

"I have to tell you something."

"Not now, Mai," he said. Just a bit farther. Was Lester with his dad? His heart pounded.

"It can't wait."

"We're almost there." At the next doorway, he could hear his dad's voice and at least one other, maybe two. Sweat greased his palms. He rubbed them on his shirt.

Mai grabbed his arm, squeezing it. "Fred."

What was wrong with her? He turned around. She looked more nervous than he was. "If you're too scared, go back up."

"No, it's not that."

Frustrated, he tried to pull away. She wouldn't let go of his arm, clutching him even tighter.

"It's about your box." Her voice was barely a whisper—a feather of sound floating into his ear.

He stopped struggling.

Her throat bobbed. She bit her lip, her eyes not quite meeting his.

"Lester doesn't have it."

"Of course he does. Wait. You think Dad has it?"

She shook her head.

"Who, then?"

Brown eyes shiny with unshed tears met his.

"Me."

Chapter 26

"*YOU* TOOK IT? YEAH, RIGHT," Fred said.

"It *was* me!"

"Why would you say that?"

"Because it's true."

"Mai, I know you didn't do it. You're just trying to stop me from following Lester."

She stomped her foot. "I took it!"

"I don't need you to protect me. Now, are you coming with me or not?"

He inched closer to the open doorway. Mai's voice faded as he concentrated on the other voices. He could almost make them out. But his heart was still beating so loudly it thudded in his ears. *Boom. Boom. Boom.* He sucked in a deep breath and let it out slowly, trying to calm down.

"Fred, I'm serious!" Mai hissed.

"Shh, I'm trying to listen."

She leaned in close to him, standing on her tiptoes and whispered into his ear. "I took it from the hole you dug under your sleeping bag."

Fred whipped around, his eyes locking with hers. He hadn't told anyone where his hiding place was. Her arm was pressed against his. He backed away and it fell to her side.

"*You* stole it from me?"

"I—"

"What did you do with it?"

"Please don't be mad."

"Mai, tell me where it is, right now."

The voices inside the room were louder, like they were moving closer to the door. Fred had a flash of panic at getting caught, then thought, *What difference does it make?* So what if Lester and his dad were in there? Lester wasn't the box thief. Mai was. He edged past her and bolted up the stairs into the daylight.

"Fred, wait." Mai was close on his heels.

He spun around. "Where is it?" he demanded.

"I don't have it here," she said gesturing to her costume. "I came right from the restaurant."

"You left it in the tent all day?" he shouted.

Mai blinked, clearly startled. Even in his anger, Fred instantly realized why—he'd never yelled at her before. Not ever.

"Why?" he asked, lowering his voice. He shook his head. It seemed like a bad dream.

Tears spilled down her cheeks. "B-because it's stealing.

You'd have gotten in trouble. That Gerard guy would have turned you in for sure."

"*It isn't stealing*!"

"You were going to s-steal those keys from the museum, too."

Fred felt as if his blood had become hot steam. "Only to see if they opened the box!" he bellowed. "I wasn't going to keep them!"

"I—I'm s-sorry," she sobbed.

"Do you still have it?"

She didn't answer, her face buried in her hands. Her shoulders were shaking.

"Geez, Fred, yell a little louder," Grace said. "I don't think the guards heard you on shore." She and Jeeter appeared from around the corner. "What's going on?"

Several passengers were watching them. He turned toward the ocean, sucking in deep breaths. Mai had betrayed him. The entire day wasted! Searching tents! This boat ride! He could have opened the box long ago—his mom could have gone home!

"Fred?"

Mai's usually sweet voice now sounded like nails on a chalkboard. He ignored her.

"I only did it to help you."

The deck tilted under his feet. The dark clouds were closer and they'd lost the sun. Waves smacked against the hull. The deep blue of the ocean was now a steely grey.

"Only did *what* to help him?" Grace said. "Why are you crying?"

Mai babbled some response. She was really crying now, hiccuping, too.

"Fred, what did you do?" Grace accused.

He felt a ripple of guilt, but immediately pushed it away. The ocean's choppy darkness matched his mood. His hip banged into the railing as the ship swayed.

They'd exited the harbour and rounded past the lighthouse. The ship was heading in the direction of Le Chameau Rock, named after the ship it had wrecked. They couldn't be going that far, though; it would take too long. Fred recognized the landmarks, having scoured every map of the area he could find before this weekend.

Fred leaned against the railing, the spray flying high as the ship cut through the waves. The rocky shoreline edged past on the left, or the port side according to the book on *Le Chameau* he'd read. The trees were obscured by ribbons of fog. A tourist paused, snapping shots of the coast.

"What's happened?" Grace asked. She stood beside him, draping her arms over the side of the boat. "Mai's a blubbering mess."

"She didn't tell you?"

"She was trying. But she wasn't making any sense. Something about the box, then crazy talk about stealing keys and prison," Grace said with a smirk. "Must be heat stroke."

"Yeah, right, that's the reason."

"Your fault." She jabbed him with her elbow. "It's because of you she worked in that restaurant inferno all afternoon."

"It's not my fault!"

"Hey, lighten up. I'm kidding."

Fred didn't bother filling Grace in on what Mai was really upset about. She'd find out what Mai had done soon enough. And he didn't feel like talking about it. The wind gave the boat wings, and they flew through the water, really moving now. It seemed like no time at all and they'd already reached the area of Little Lorraine.

Three large longboats were heading from shore toward them. A booming voice echoed through the ship. "We'll be dropping anchor and the second part of the adventure will begin!"

There was scattered applause.

"You'll be leaving the *Invictum* and the longboats will take you ashore for a brief excursion to a site where the British landed. Refreshments are planned at sunset and then buses will return you to the fortress."

Leave now? Was this planned? No one looked surprised. It must be part of the tour. Was his dad leaving too?

Fred returned to the other side of the ship, where they'd come aboard. Already, the tourists had started lining up. "Uh, what did we come on this boat for?" Grace said. "We didn't even do anything and now we're getting off."

Jeeter was with Mai, standing close to the line. Grace went over to them and said something. Jeeter glanced over at Fred, but Mai's head was bowed, her hair covering her face.

The crew leapt amongst the rigging, pulling in the sails and tying them tight. The ship groaned and creaked, again reminding Fred of something alive. This time it was cranky at being bound, probably feeling strangled like he did in his shirt and tie on Sundays. It wanted to run. Be free.

The ship slowed noticeably and dropped anchor with a huge splash. They'd soon be disembarking. Remaining stragglers appeared and joined the line. One of the boats drew alongside. Ropes were thrown down to tie it on while the passengers descended the ladder.

The crowd clustered together, shuffling forward like a herd of sheep. Mai moved closer to them. If she was getting off, so was he. If she still had the box, he couldn't let her go back alone. She'd turn it in.

That was not happening.

But where was his dad? Then it hit him. Of course! They were getting everyone off the ship. His dad would stay on board so he could dive undetected.

Well, there wasn't anything he could do about that. The box was more important. More important than anything his dad was going to try to haul up from the bottom of the sea, that was for sure. And his dad would come up empty-handed anyway, like always. Fred moved to stand in line.

Then Molly, park archaeologist and harbourmaster, wished the group of people she was talking to a good time and walked away—toward the back of the ship. She was staying on board?

Fred remembered what she'd said earlier—no one can dive without a permit from her. His father's night dive flashed in his mind. There was no way he had a permit.

Chapter 27

WHAT WOULD MOLLY DO? WOULD his dad get arrested? Would he go to prison? He couldn't let that happen. But he couldn't let Mai give his box away, either. He had to keep her on the ship.

"Grace," he said, motioning with his hand.

She pointed to the line, now doubly long as it filled with crew. They must be going on the shore excursion for the free food. His stomach growled. Could he ask them to bring him back a doggy bag? He waved at Grace again. Scowling, she stormed over. "What now?"

"We can't get off."

"Why not?"

"Because Molly, that archaeologist from the museum, isn't getting off, either. She might be after Dad. We have to warn him."

Grace's eyebrows shot up. "Do you know what he's up to?"

"Not exactly. But I bet he doesn't have a permit, whatever it is."

Grace didn't hesitate, slapping him on the shoulder. "No sweat. Be right back." She jogged over to Jeeter and Mai, who were in a deep discussion. She put an arm around each one's shoulders, creating a huddle.

Whatever she said worked. Mai and Jeeter followed her as she strolled back across the deck. "Okay, they're in," she said.

Mai glanced at him with her red, swollen eyes, but didn't say anything. Jeeter had his hand at her elbow and shot Fred a nasty look. Not exactly all-for-one-and-one-for-all attitudes, but at least they had stayed on board.

Grace put her hands on her hips. "Are we just going to stand here?"

"Hang on," Fred said. He wanted to get over to the port side of the ship. And from there, back to the entrance to below decks, which was inside the captain's cabin. But it wasn't as simple as strolling straight across. The foredeck was pretty wide open, with only a few places for cover—lifeboats, barrels, and crates, that kind of stuff.

If Molly saw them, she'd want to know why they were still on the ship. Fred definitely didn't want to run into her before his dad. So he chose the route with the best cover. He crouched down and scuttled along the railing to the stern until they were behind the captain's cabin. Here, they were hidden from the rest of the ship and from any crew, who would be sure to herd them to the departing boats.

The four of them huddled together. Mai had squeezed close to Jeeter, and, Fred noticed, as far from Fred as possible. That was fine by him.

They waited several long minutes in silence.

If anyone came around either side, they'd be toast. There was nowhere to go. They were sitting ducks. Fred noticed he kept holding his breath and tried to relax. He could feel adrenaline coursing through him. It felt like a game of hide-and-seek, with much higher stakes than being tagged. And in the worst hiding place. Ever.

"Freddo, man, let's get on with it already."

"Shh," Fred hissed back.

"Jeeter's right," Grace said. "We can't stay here forever."

"Fine!" Fred poked his head around the side of the captain's cabin, back the way they'd come. The line was gone. Shouted orders indicated the longboats were away. He scurried over and checked the other corner. That part of the deck was clear, too. It was now or never.

"You guys stay here. Back in a sec."

He sidled along the wall. Pushing his back against it as he went, he willed himself to be invisible. Where had Molly gone? Below decks? Was his dad still down there? He reached the doorway to the captain's cabin and once more descended the stairs.

He heard nothing at first. But someone had to be down here. Unless they were all in the captain's cabin. But he'd heard no voices upstairs, either. Frustrated and feeling as if he was running out of time, he let go of caution and strode boldly to the end of the hall, where he'd heard his dad last time. A door was open.

He paused, listening. There was a low hum of voices. He crept closer.

"He's going down now," a muffled female voice said. It sounded like Molly, the archaeologist. "Lester's with him."

Fred inched forward.

"And he's okay with it?" a male voice replied. "I know Pete. I didn't think he'd go for it."

"He doesn't know."

"What do you mean?" the man asked.

"He thinks it's all part of his skills assessment for a scuba diver position at the fortress." Molly laughed. "He doesn't know about Lester either."

"Oh, that's rich!" the guy cackled. "So he's finding all these treasure sites for you and he thinks it's for a job?"

"I know. I'm a genius," Molly said. "But don't think it fell into my lap. I've been living in this awful place for a year lining this up. It wasn't without sacrifice. I'm not sailing around the world, captain of a tall ship, like you."

"Pretty slick, Molly. I'm impressed."

"I couldn't have done it without him. He knows more than anyone about treasure hunting around here. But what he knew wasn't doing him any good alone. He couldn't get anywhere near these sites without permits, which are impossible to get."

"Lucky for you his business went under when it did. He doesn't strike me as the type that likes to work for anyone but himself."

"You think it was *luck*?"

There was a pause. "You sabotaged his business? That's cold, even for you, Molly."

"Too much at stake—we only had a brief window here with the encampment and the tall ships. I wasn't taking any chances. A few phone calls to the right people, and his contracts dried up overnight. Of course, Lester was in place for a while. I had him make contact some time ago."

Fred could feel his legs shaking. His hands were clenched so tight he was cutting off the circulation in his fingers. Lester had betrayed his dad. And this woman had ruined his dad's business? Was anyone who they seemed?

"And something else—quite unexpected. Pete had told me his son and friends were here. He was still being quite secretive about his dive sites and wasn't letting Lester go with him until today. So I had Lester and a rather overenthusiastic guard from the fortress keep an eye on the kids. I wasn't leaving anything to chance."

Fred sucked in a breath. So he hadn't been paranoid. Molly had Lester and Gerard spying on them!

"Pete's son is apparently a treasure hunter, too," Molly continued. "He found a box buried at the fortress. His little girlfriend was terrified he'd get found out and brought it to me just this afternoon. A nice little bonus, I'd say."

Mai *had* turned in his box. His nails dug into his hands and a muscle twitched in his eye. How could she have done it?

"A box?" the man said.

"Here, I'll show you." There was a clanging noise.

"What else you got in there?"

"Some lovely trinkets Pete found on his dives. The main extraction of the artifacts will take place over the next few weeks, of course, after he gives me the exact coordinates. But that will have to be done with the submersible."

"You've got a *sub*?" There was awe in the man's voice.

"Oh, we've got all the toys," Molly said. "It's a small one, rented from a government oceanic institute. For *research*, of course. Still costs a small fortune! But that's no problem. These Europeans will pay anything to get their artifacts back."

"Doesn't look like much," the guy said.

Fred crept to the very edge of the doorjamb. A set of keys dangled from the lock. He peered inside. Molly held a duffle bag open and the captain was examining Fred's box.

"The boy thinks there are jewels inside." Molly shrugged. "But it's welded shut. Might be nothing. Or something. Won't know 'til we get it open."

"I think I've got a blowtorch around here somewhere."

Fred's pulse quickened. He was fighting every instinct to rush in and rip his box from the captain. But now he might finally see what's inside.

The captain rooted through a couple of tool boxes in the corner. "Aha!" he said. "I knew I had one here somewhere." He lit the torch.

FARROOOSH!

Fred held his breath, his eyes glued to the blue-orange flame.

"Just at the very end, there, should do it," Molly said. "Don't want to ruin anything flammable inside."

The captain expertly focused the flame on the side of the box, directing the flame to its edge. He worked the torch slowly around the side.

"Almost there!" he said. "Let me cool it off a bit first." He stuck the non-cut portion of the box into a bucket at his feet. It sizzled and steam shot upward. He let it sit there for a minute, then pulled it back out, testing the metal with his hand. "That's better."

"Let's see what we've got," Molly said, leaning closer.

The captain restarted the torch.

Fred gasped. *No!*

The captain's head jerked at the noise. He met Fred's eyes and recoiled, apparently shocked to see someone standing there. The box clattered to the ground.

"What are you doing?" Molly said to the captain.

Fred dove through the doorway and scooped the box from the floor. The captain seemed to move in slow motion, reaching for Fred after he'd already zigzagged out of the way. Molly hadn't been facing the door, and she looked shocked as he yanked the duffle bag from her hands.

Her eyes locked with his and her pupils widened in recognition. "You!"

Chapter 28

FRED CONTINUED IN A CIRCLE around Molly and raced out the door, her curses following him. He slammed it shut and jerked the key in the lock.

Heart pounding, he leaned against the closed door. It took a moment to sink in. He had the box. It was still very warm. Its left end was almost totally cut. One good smack against something should—

BANG!

Fred's body shook, mirroring the door's vibrations.

"Open this door, you little troll!" Molly shrieked.

The door shuddered again.

Fred backed away from it and noticed the keys still dangling from the lock. He grabbed them and turned and bolted down the hall and up the stairs. He slammed that door shut, too. That captain guy would get them out in no time. He had to lock it, and fast.

Fred tried several keys. His hands shook. Footsteps thundered from below. He tried another key. It didn't fit. Molly's screaming rants were getting closer. Fred peered in the window. The captain was running up the stairs.

Fred dropped the keys. He stopped breathing.

It was over.

He couldn't help himself, looking in the window again. The captain was now at the top of the stairs. Molly was right behind him.

He gulped and scooped up the keys. Closing his eyes and praying, he slid another key in the lock. It fit. As Fred turned it, he looked up. The captain was right there! The handle rattled. It was locked. The captain banged on the glass, his eyes wild.

The door held.

"Grace," Fred yelled, "come on!"

Three heads appeared from behind the captain's cabin. Each of them had the same questioning look on their face.

"Hurry up!"

"We're coming, take it easy," Grace said.

"We've got to get off this boat. Now!"

"A little late for that," Jeeter said. "You got us out of the line, remember? Our ride is gone." He pointed toward shore.

He'd forgotten! Desperately, his eyes roamed the deck. "The lifeboat!"

"Are you kidding me, man?" Jeeter said. "What's going on? Why are we leaving a perfectly good, non-sinking ship to get on a lifeboat?"

"It's all a scam. Molly's a crook! And she's using Dad. I

just stole my box back and a bag of Dad's artifacts and she is majorly ticked. So is that captain guy. If we don't get off, and I mean *now*, we're done for!"

Fred ran to the foredeck. The lifeboat was perched on a platform. It was perfect. They just had to get it in the water. He tugged on the side. It didn't budge. Frowning, he pulled harder. Nothing.

It must be stuck on something. He stepped back, examining it from stem to stern. It seemed to be in good condition. It didn't look like a prop. He ran his hand down the hull. Crap! It was bolted to the deck. No wonder he couldn't move it.

Now what? Fred thought of the blowtorch below decks. That would get through the bolts. The only problems were the crazy-eyed captain and demented archaeologist between him and it. Not an option.

"We're not getting off in that," Grace said.

"No kidding," Fred barked.

"You see those long white tubes?" Jeeter pointed to them lining each side of the deck. "Those are the operational life rafts."

"Well, let's get one open. Fast!"

"Are you sure about that?" Jeeter said. "The captain will kill you. It'll cost a fortune to get the raft repacked and certified again. You'll have to pay for it."

Fred cackled crazily. "The captain already wants to kill me, for real!"

"It can't be that bad. A few trinkets don't equal murder," Grace said. "Where's your dad? He'll straighten this out."

Of course! He ran to the railing. Another thunderhead darkened the sky. Two heads with scuba masks bobbed in the water. Fred waved his arms frantically, trying to get his dad's attention. One diver adjusted the mask down over his face.

"Dad!" he shouted.

But his voice must have been lost on the wind. The heads disappeared beneath the choppy waves.

He was too late. His dad was now underwater with Lester, his traitorous friend.

BANG!

The door to the captain's cabin rattled again. No way was it going to hold them for very long. The only options were to hide or get off the boat. And the only place to hide was below decks. They had no choice. It had to be the life raft.

"How do we get it open?"

"Man, are you sure about this?" Jeeter asked. "Those waves are rockin'. It's not far to the shore, but—"

"A life raft? That's not a real boat! The waves are getting so high. What if it tips over?" Mai squeaked.

"If the captain and Molly get out, we'll have more to worry about than a life raft. She's running a scam. Trying to get treasure from the shipwrecks, illegally." He held up the heavy duffle bag. "And she ruined Dad's business. Who knows how far she'll go."

"I can't believe she's a criminal!" Mai cried. "And I can't believe I gave her your box."

Fred patted the bag. "Safe and sound, remember?"

Jeeter pulled a lever from the underside of the tube. "Get ready." The tube split open. They dragged the uninflated boat a short distance to where the ladder hung over the side of the *Invictum* so they'd be able to climb down to board the raft.

A cord dangled from the side of the raft. Fred reached over and pulled it.

"Not yet!" Jeeter yelled.

The raft hissed and puffed.

The ship swayed, knocked about by the now-high waves. The raft snapped open, half over the railing.

"Grab it!" Jeeter cried.

Fred lunged for one of the ropes. But it was too late to stop it. Lightning flashed and rain exploded from the thunderhead now directly overhead. The raft tumbled over the side, dragging Fred with it.

Thunder crashed as he plunged into the freezing water.

Chapter 29

THE RAFT BUOYED, WHILE FRED dropped like a stone. One hand was frozen around the handles of the duffle bag. His other stretched above his head, still clutching the rope from the raft.

Kicking his feet, Fred tried to slow his descent. But the bag was like an anchor, determined to get to the ocean floor. He continued to be pulled down. His arm ached, his muscles straining.

The murky water churned, and long strands of kelp swirled and tangled around him. His lungs burned, craving oxygen. The line jerked and he stopped. The end of the rope! His hand slid.

He couldn't hold it. Below, the hazy, rocky bottom beckoned. It might be his only chance. Closing his eyes, Fred let go of the rope. And sank. His lungs were on fire.

Hitting the bottom, he felt around inside the duffle bag and grabbed his box.

Monsieur Fornac, the merchant, hadn't been able to abandon his treasure. It had cost him his life. His bones were somewhere close by in this very ocean. Fred knew he had no choice. Not if he wanted to live.

He released the bag, still holding the box, and pushed off with his feet, shooting back up toward the surface. He kicked as hard as he could. Pain ripped through his chest. Air. He needed air. Stars exploded behind his eyes.

The instinct to open his mouth was overwhelming. A breath. One breath. But if he did that, he was dead. Fred clamped his lips tighter. The closer he got to the surface, the slower he seemed to go. It was like swimming in glue. Concrete arms. Granite legs. He wasn't going to make it.

Let go of the box.

No! He clutched it tighter, his legs moving, but only in imitations of kicks now. Maybe he was just like Fornac after all. His mom's face swam in front of him. She was smiling, eyes bright with happiness and health. He reached toward her. His fingers brushed against something and instinctively curled around it. The rope from the raft.

Fred shot upward.

Rain pelted his face. He sucked in air. Drank it. Sweet, sweet air. His lungs were sails, filled and billowing with air. A wave crashed over his head and he gulped a mouthful of seawater. Hands reached out and grabbed his shirt. He was lifted up, out of the water. He tumbled into the raft.

Lying there, Fred coughed out seawater, and sucked in breath after breath. He couldn't get enough.

"We thought you were a goner!" Grace's voice shook.

"I almost was," Fred croaked.

"Thank Jeeter," Grace said. "He grabbed the line when we got in the lifeboat and wouldn't let go. As soon as he felt you tug on it, he pulled you up."

Fred looked over at Jeeter. "Thanks." One word. One word in exchange for saving his life. It didn't seem to be enough.

Jeeter grinned. "No problem, Freddo. You are one crazy dude!"

Being called Freddo didn't grate on his nerves this time. Fred even managed a grin. A real one. He leaned back, resting his head against the side of the raft. He pulled his box to his chest. Everyone else was as wet as he was. Water from the thundershower sloshed around his feet.

"I'm glad you're safe," Mai said. Sitting in the front of the raft, she had her arms wrapped around her knees. Her eyes were even redder than before. She'd been crying again.

"Thanks," he mumbled.

"I thought—I thought. I mean, we couldn't see you." She sniffed, her eyes welling up again.

With his box clutched safely in his arms, Fred didn't feel quite so angry. Mai had only done what she did to protect him. He knew that.

Mai smiled through her tears.

Fred's gaze was drawn to the anchored ship. They'd drifted quite a way from it now, their raft close to shore.

No one was visible on deck. Would Molly still come for them? She'd have to use the other life raft. There wasn't enough crew on the *Invictum* to sail it.

Sunlight flickered, punching its way through the clouds. Although the sun was low on the horizon, traces of blue still speckled the sky. The anvil-shaped thundercloud continued to throw its temper tantrum, but farther out at sea.

Fred examined his box. The end was almost off. He might be able to twist it.

"The suspense is killing me!" Grace said. "Open it already!"

Fred hesitated. Unease mushroomed in his gut. What if it wasn't what he thought? He held his breath and wiggled the cut end. It wasn't coming off without a fight. There wasn't anything in the raft he could use. He needed a rock or something to smack it on.

"*EEEK!*"

Fred's head whipped up at Mai's scream. A black-gloved hand was clutching the raft beside her. A masked head appeared.

"Dad?" Fred said.

His dad nodded, pulling off his scuba mask. "What are you kids doing here? We surfaced closer to the ship. Lester was climbing on board when I spotted you. Where did you get the raft?"

"From the ship," Fred said. "Dad, I've got to tell you something."

"You were on the ship?" His head swivelled in that direction. "Why?"

"Dad, Molly's a crook!"

"You know Molly?" He looked confused.

"Not really, but—"

"Geez, son, you can't say things like that about people."

"Dad, I heard her. She's getting your dive sites for some people that want to steal all the treasure. She's been planning it for a year."

"What?" His dad's face had gone grey. "But the job…"

Fred reached out and grabbed his dad's arm. "There's no job, Dad. She was using you. Her position at the fortress is a cover. Your friend Lester's even in on it. It's all a scam."

"Scam? Lester?" His father's voice was barely a whisper.

"That's not the worst." Fred cleared his throat. "Umm… she…"

"Not the worst? What could be worse?" His father's voice cracked. "All this time, wasted. What are we going to do now? Your mother…" He sank lower in the water, his forehead resting on the edge of the raft.

"No, Dad, it's okay," Fred said. He crawled over to him, deciding not to add that Molly had also deliberately wrecked his business. "Don't worry, we'll be all right. I've got treasure."

His dad lifted his head. "What treasure?"

"For Mom." Fred held out the box. "It'll take care of everything."

"What are you talking about?'

"But I have to get it open. Don't happen to have a rock with you, do you?"

His dad rose up, towering above the raft. "No, but there's a few thousand to choose from." He pointed behind Fred.

The raft had drifted into Little Lorraine Harbour's beach. His father pushed it the last few feet. Rocks scraped the bottom as Fred hopped out, his bare feet splashing in the shallow water. His wet wool pants stuck to his legs. The white shirt sagged, water still dripping from the elbows.

"Now, are you going to tell me what's going on? This life raft—you got it from the ship? Do you know how much trouble you kids can get in for that?" His father had taken off his scuba gear and was pulling off his fins.

"The captain and Molly were chasing me," Fred said. "I locked them in the captain's cabin. But we had to get off the ship before they broke free."

"Locked up? Chasing you?" His father's eyes darkened. "I think I better get the whole story, not bits and pieces. Start from the beginning."

Fred sighed, sitting on the edge of the raft, and proceeded to spill his guts. First about the box, and then the events on the ship.

"So, let me understand this. You think that box belonged to an ancestor and is full of jewels? Are you serious, son?"

"I'm sure of it, Dad. It was in his journal. All about how he got them. And then later, when he went to the Fortress of Louisbourg as an adult, and how he hid them before the siege."

His dad didn't look convinced. "Well, let's have a look."

Fred scanned the shore, picking a tall boulder several metres away. His stomach was flipping and tripping along with his bare feet as he gingerly navigated the small rocks and seaweed. Mai, Grace, Jeeter, and his dad circled around the boulder.

He held the box over his head and brought it down fast, smacking it as hard as he could on a jagged edge of the boulder.

PIINGG!

Vibrations shot up his arm. The box sailed out of his hands and fell into the water. The contents had gone flying, too, ricocheting off the rock and into Fred's leg. A pouch the size of a squished softball sat at his feet.

Everyone's eyes were glued to it.

Holding his breath, Fred picked it up and opened the drawstring. He stuck his hand inside and pulled out a roll made of brown leather, just like the pouch. It was still soft, protected by the sealed box. And it seemed to be treated with some kind of oil. He spread it open in his palm. Lining the inside of the roll were several pockets stitched in the leather.

His fingers trembled as he checked the first pocket, pulling out what lay inside. It was the size of a quarter. Fading sunlight reflected off the ruby's deep red edges.

His father gasped.

"Jewels!" Grace squealed. "I can't believe it. Real treasure!"

Fred emptied the remaining pockets. Green, blue, red, white, and yellow—a gemstone rainbow.

"Yellow diamond," his father said. He held it up. "Magnificent!"

"What are they worth?" Jeeter asked.

"Hundreds of thousands, at least."

Fred gawked at his dad. "Seriously?"

His father nodded. "I'm no expert, but this one diamond has got to be at least twenty or thirty carats, maybe more. A high-quality five-carat diamond can run as high as a hundred thousand dollars. And you've got a couple of dozen gemstones here."

"We're rich!" Fred yelped.

Chapter 30

THE BUS RIDE BACK TO the fortress was uneventful. Fred kept expecting Molly to try and overtake them—some kind of a supervillain chase scene. But they bumped along the old warped highway from Little Lorraine to Louisbourg at a plodding, uninterrupted pace.

From the beach, Mai had noticed the buses coming down the hill on the highway—the group of tourists from the ship. They'd happily allowed Fred and the rest of them to hitch a ride. As they'd boarded, his dad had looked back out toward the harbour. The longboats filled with crew had returned to the *Invictum*.

Unlike the school bus, where the back seats were premium real estate, all the tourists were sitting toward the front. Fred had made a beeline for the back two empty rows where they huddled together. Mai was fidgeting and Fred knew the fact that he intended to keep the jewels was eating her up.

The drive was mostly silent, after Fred had asked his dad about Lester. Turns out he was an old diving buddy who had shown up a while ago and had wanted his dad to try and get him a job at the fortress too. All lies, as it turned out.

But Fred's thoughts had not rested long on Lester. His mind was flying on super-speed—on a jewel-studded racetrack. He'd sell some of the gemstones immediately, enough so that his mom could get top medical treatment. Dad could get his business running again. They'd even get a new house. And a new computer. Oh, and a new bike. And enough chocolate to fill a hundred backpacks. He'd get a fridge for his room just for his chocolate and cola. He groaned as his stomach growled.

They arrived back at the fortress and his dad immediately went to the security office. Fred had wanted to go with him, but his dad had refused. He'd insisted that Fred stay out of it.

So they waited. And waited. Fred's legs were twitching. His fist was clutched around his pouch of jewels. What if they didn't believe the story? It was kind of out there. And what proof did they have?

Two men and a woman hurried by them, and entered the same office his dad had been in for ages. The door shut firmly behind them. That didn't seem good.

But his dad hadn't done anything wrong! Could they get in trouble for the life raft? It's not like they'd stolen it. And the ship wasn't part of the fortress, anyway. Would the shady captain dare to complain? The longer the wait, the worse it seemed.

"They've been in there forever," Grace whispered. "What do you suppose is taking so long?"

"I don't know," Fred said. "Maybe they don't believe him. I mean, what evidence is there? Just the word of some kids!"

As he said it, he realized how crazy this probably seemed to someone who hadn't been there. It sounded like a wild, made-up story. These people didn't even know his dad. But they'd known Molly for a whole year. And she had played the part perfectly. Fred shivered, thinking how nice she'd seemed.

He fidgeted and itched like crazy in the damp, stinky wool pants, and tried to return to his daydreams about the new life his jewels would bring. They'd never have to worry about money. His mom would get better. He pictured her sitting out on their new deck overlooking the water, smiling.

But then his thoughts kept switching back to his dad. What would happen to him? Molly knew about the box. What if she said something—made an anonymous tip? Or she could try and use the information to make a deal or something if they caught her. His dad would get arrested for sure. Probably Fred, too. What if they were arresting his dad right now? He clutched the leather pouch tighter.

"I have to do something!" Fred stood up and began walking toward the closed door. He couldn't believe it. Part of him was screaming in his head that he was nuts, and to turn around. The other part of him wasn't too sure what he was doing, either.

"Where are you going?" Grace cried. "Your dad said to let him handle it."

"I can't. They won't believe him. I'll have to tell them!"

He opened the door. Everyone was sitting around a conference table. Two had laptops in front of them. They all looked up. Fred's legs began to shake.

"Let him go!" Fred's heart thumped, banging so loudly it felt as if it was going to explode out of his chest.

"Fred, I told you to stay out of this," his dad said. "I can handle it."

"That Molly person is a crook! She tricked my dad. She made his business go under so he'd have no choice but to work for her. She's going to steal all the treasure from the wrecks!"

His dad's face went white at the mention of his business.

"And...and...if you let my dad go, I'll give you these!" He held up the bag. His hand was shaking. *What am I doing? They still haven't seen anything. I can turn around and leave right now and they won't find out. We could still be rich.*

"Son—"

"No, Dad, " Fred said. His voice cracked. "You can't go to jail!"

"Jail?" the lady closest to his dad asked.

"He's the good guy," Fred said. "And he's a great diver. He knows all the wrecks. You should have hired him. You'd be lucky to have him! He—"

"Listen here, young man!" a stern-looking grey-haired man said.

"Let Dad go and...and..." Fred choked on the words, but he continued, "...you can have them." He turned the pouch upside down, shaking it. He clenched his other fist tightly to his side, to stop it from reaching out to grab them. The jewels spilled across the table.

Everyone gasped.

—

The campfire flickered. It was late. The fortress was eerily quiet, the campers and staff now sleeping.

His mom and dad had wanted to take them home, but they were stuck at the fortress for the night. Heavy rainfall from the thunderstorms had flooded the lower roads out of town, and the hotels were booked solid with tourists. Extra staff were patrolling the grounds in case Molly or Lester showed up and tried to cause trouble.

Fred, his parents, Mai, Grace, and Jeeter were all sitting in a circle around their firepit. Fred felt empty. He'd barely held the jewels, but it was as if part of him had gone with them. Had he done the right thing? Not that it mattered now. It was done.

Fred's mom was sitting beside his dad and he had his arm around her. He leaned over and whispered in her ear. She laughed. It tinkled, like a bell, floating on the air. Fred's breath caught. She looked happy…and almost like she used to. A trick of the glowing fire.

Fred was still bursting to hear what had happened after he'd made the grand gesture and turned in the jewels. His dad had remained inside for a long time after Fred had been asked to leave the room. Then security guards had escorted them back to their site, so there hadn't been any chance to talk. He couldn't stand it any longer. He had to get some answers.

"So, did they believe you?" Fred asked. "About Molly?"

His dad took the can of cola Jeeter held out and popped the tab. He took a long drink. "Not at first."

"What changed their minds?" Grace asked.

"They checked her email account. It was all there on the park's computer."

"Wow, that wasn't too smart," Jeeter said.

"I guess after a year she'd gotten comfortable," his dad said with a shrug. "Lucky break for us. Otherwise, it would have been hard to prove. But they think there's enough evidence to take to the police for fraud. She's probably long gone by now, though."

"But won't she still be able to take the treasure from the wrecks?" Fred asked.

His dad shook his head. "I never gave her the exact coordinates. I brought up samples to prove I knew where they were, but was waiting to get officially hired before I shared that information. Lester was on that last dive with me, so they know that site. But the fortress is going to monitor it. Besides, she booked all the equipment using her fortress title. Not much she can do without that cover. Everyone knows the area is part of the government park."

Mai turned to Fred. "And you really gave them your treasure?"

Fred nodded.

"I'm so proud of you," Mai said. "You did the right thing."

"I don't know about that," Fred said.

"I do," his mom said. "It *was* the right thing to do, Freddy." She beamed at him.

"Yeah, but we're still broke!"

"Not for long," his dad said. "They offered me a job."

"They did?" Fred said.

"They want to excavate all the wrecks I mapped. And number one on the list is the site Lester knows. I'll be running the whole program." He winked at Fred. "I think it was your endorsement that sealed the deal. And maybe that fortune in gems didn't hurt, either. It'll fund the entire project, maybe more!"

His dad had a job! He thought of his dad's fake job prospects from Molly. "Dad, why didn't you tell me why you were here? That you were trying to get a job? All this time, I thought..." He drifted off, not able to say the rest out loud.

His dad grimaced. "I couldn't. I've had so many things go wrong, so many screwups, especially lately." His voice became gruff. "I couldn't say anything until I knew for certain. I didn't want another disappointment. For you or for your mother."

His mom leaned over and kissed his dad. Fred stood up, walked over to his parents, and enveloped them both in a hug.

The whole group stayed there, chatting and laughing while the fire went from crackling flames to smouldering coals. His dad's new job, and what it would mean for their family, began to sink in. And the fact that Fred had made it happen. He laughed more than he had in weeks. He even joked around with Jeeter. His feelings of being a dumb kid in kindergarten evaporated in the campfire's curling smoke.

Eventually, droopy eyes and yawns overtook the chatter. Jeeter went back to his tent, Mai and Grace to theirs. His parents settled in as well. Fred was bunking with Jeeter, and slowly made his way over to the tent, where Jeeter was already snoring. He tossed down his sleeping bag on the empty side and lay down for a while. But he remained wide awake, his head bursting with the events of the day. Realizing he wasn't going to sleep, he gave up and went back outside.

Fred sat on the quay wall, his legs dangling. The moonlight shimmered on the still water. Slowly, he pulled an aged piece of parchment from his shorts pocket. It had been in the box when Fred had retrieved it from the water. Wrapped tightly in leather, it had also been protected.

Fred gazed at it and grinned.

His very own treasure map.

Acknowledgements

MY LIST OF PEOPLE TO thank seems to expand with each book. I am grateful to all of you who take an interest and share in this part of my life.

Thanks so much to my growing list of beta readers—Amy McCarron, Lisa Smith, Peggy Laidlaw, Mary McCarron, Rhonda Basden, Judy Bailey, Sandy Denny, Hélène Dahl, Tyler Grant, Maude Bailey, and Brian Basden, I appreciate your commitment of time and that you enjoy being part of the process.

Thanks to my dear friends and writing group members Daphne Greer, Lisa Harrington, Jennifer Thorne, Graham Bullock, and Joanna Butler. You keep the wheels moving forward. Sounds easy, but it isn't.

My family is an ongoing source of support and encouragement. Thanks to James, Mom, Dad, Paulette, Will, Dave, Shari, Mary, Matthew, and Ella.

Thanks also to the editing family at Nimbus, especially Penelope, for her pursuit of perfection.

And to the students, teachers, and library staff I visit each year—it's a joy to share my stories with you.